Camp Club Girls

Alexis
AND THE

ARIZONA ESCAPADE

Cover design: Thinkpen Design

Published by Barbour Publishing, Inc., P.O. Box 719, Uhrichsville, Ohio 44683, www.barbourbooks.com

Our mission is to publish and distribute inspirational products offering exceptional value and biblical encouragement to the masses.

Member of the
Evangelical Christian
Publishers Association

Printed in the United States of America.

Dickinson Press, Grand Rapids, MI; August 2010; D10002448

Camp Club Girls

Alexis
AND THE
ARIZONA
ESCAPADE

Erica Rodgers

BARBOUR
PUBLISHING

CHAPTER 1

The Bridge in the Desert

The noon sun shone bright in a sapphire sky. But twelve-year-old Alexis Howell wasn't paying attention. She stood on the bridge and watched the Arizona heat warping the hills of sand and sagebrush in the distance.

She had never been so afraid in all her life.

Alexis made herself look at the clouds to try to keep her mind off her fear. She liked their shapes, but mostly she was keeping her mind off the water. A crowd of tourists clamored past, and a tall man bumped her into the rail. Her eyes were ripped from the sky as she caught her balance. . .and looked down.

It seemed like forever to the water below. The wind blew, lifting her brown ponytail. The bridge swayed. It rocked beneath her feet.

Maybe it will flip over and throw me off, Alexis thought in sudden panic.

Why had she promised to meet Elizabeth *here* of all places? Why?

Like most children, Alexis had grown up singing the song "London Bridge is falling down. . . ." She'd certainly been surprised to learn that the London Bridge wasn't in London at all. It was here in Arizona.

Another group of tourists nudged past. A large purse landed with a *thud* against Alexis's back, and before she knew it, she had flipped forward. She screamed. She was falling. . .falling. . .falling. . . .

"Alexis?"

The vision evaporated. Alexis turned toward the voice that had said her name.

"Elizabeth! I'm so glad you're here!" She hugged her friend but then couldn't seem to let go. She clung to her friend like a life preserver.

"I'm glad, too," said Elizabeth in her soft Texas twang, not seeming to notice the tightness of the hug. "This place is beautiful! The water is so calm and peaceful, and the bridge is magnificent! I *did* think it would be bigger though."

"Sure," said Alexis, who thought the bridge was quite big enough. She released Elizabeth but then held her arm until they reached the sidewalk at the end of the bridge.

The sounds of vacation echoed off the lake. Laughing children, scolding parents, and the sputter of motorboats.

Vendors called out, advertising their wares.

"Cotton candy!"

"Funnel cakes here!"

"Hot dogs! Fresh, cold lemonade!"

Alexis had stopped shaking. Now she was simply trying to keep up with Elizabeth. This was not always easy, since her friend's legs seemed twice as long as hers. Elizabeth kept pulling on the bottom edges of her shorts, like they were too short.

"How was the trip?" said Alexis.

"Long," said Elizabeth. "We drove. We just got here, but I needed a break from my brother. Mom said I could meet you and hang out until dinner."

"Great! I'll take you to my hotel. You won't believe it. . . . It looks like a *castle*! It has an amazing pool, too. And Grandma got our room for free!"

"Wow!" said Elizabeth. "How'd she do that?"

"She's teaching some classes about British history," said Alexis. "It's a new addition to the London Bridge Days Festival." She gestured to all of the tourists.

They had entered the area of Lake Havasu City that looked like an old English village. People everywhere were dressed up. They all wore a lot of clothes for such a hot day. The women dressed in bright, heavy, velvet clothes. Some wore tattered dark clothes to look like beggars and paupers, poor people. Others were dressed regally to look like princes and queens. They reminded Alexis of the scenes and actors from movies like *Robin Hood* or *The Princess Bride* or even a few of the scenes in *The Chronicles of Narnia*.

Elizabeth turned and looked again at the bridge. She pulled her cell phone out of her pocket and took a picture. "That's really the London Bridge, huh?" asked Elizabeth.

Alexis glanced over her shoulder and shivered.

"Yep. The city of London had to replace it because it was so old, but they didn't want to throw it away, so they sold it to Lake Havasu City."

"I thought the London Bridge was tall, you know? With towers at the ends," said Elizabeth.

"You're thinking of the Tower Bridge," said Alexis. "My grandma told me that people always get them mixed up."

This bridge definitely didn't have towers. It was wide and low to the water, with five long arches supporting its weight. The top of the bridge had a stone rail that held a few old lampposts and a flagpole.

"It's so weird to see something called the London Bridge in the middle of the Arizona desert!" said Elizabeth.

Alexis laughed as she led her friend toward the London Bridge Resort, where she was staying. She was so excited to be on fall break. She had a whole week off from school, so her grandmother had invited Alexis to join her at the resort. Alexis was happy already, but she became super-excited when she found out that Elizabeth was coming, too. Elizabeth's dad came to Lake Havasu every year for the bass-fishing tournament. This year he brought the whole family.

Alexis couldn't wait to spend an entire five days with the oldest of the Camp Club Girls! Who knew? Maybe they would get a chance to solve a mystery. Something was bound to happen when crowds this large got together.

"Wow! You're staying *here*?" Elizabeth cried. They had turned into the entrance of the London Bridge Resort. Two huge towers guarded the doors. Every time Alexis looked at them, she expected to see a princess waving from the top or a dragon at the bottom, clawing to get in.

"Hey, stand by the entrance and let me get a picture," Elizabeth directed. "Then I'll send it to the rest of the Camp Club Girls."

Alexis posed until Elizabeth said, "Okay. That'll make them wish they were here."

Then Alexis led the way through the front doors, and a huge scarlet lobby glittered before them. To the left was an expanse of marble floor, which led over to the check-in desk, and to the right was—

Elizabeth gasped.

"I know," said Alexis. "Isn't it awesome?"

An expanse of soft red carpet was surrounded by gold stands and scarlet ropes. Inside the ropes was a gigantic carriage. It looked like it was made of gold. The roof of the carriage was held up by eight golden palm trees, and at the very top sat three cherubs. They were holding up the royal crown.

The girls were leaning in to get a closer look when a boyish voice snapped behind them.

"Can't you see the ropes? No touching!"

Alexis spun around. An officer in a brown sheriff's uniform stood at the edge of the carpet, crossing his arms.

"We weren't going to touch it, sir," said Elizabeth. "I promise—"

"I know troublemakers when I see 'em," said the young man. He couldn't have been much older than twenty.

"Hi," muttered Alexis. She glanced at his badge. "Um, Mr. Dewayne."

He pointed to his badge and said, "*Deputy* Dewayne to you."

"Nice to meet you," said Elizabeth, but it came out more like a question.

"Don't get smart with me, little girl!" said Deputy Dewayne. Alexis smiled. Elizabeth was easily as tall as the officer. "This is my town! I won't have tourists making a mess of things!"

Alexis and Elizabeth simply nodded.

"If I see you even put one finger over those ropes"— he pointed toward the carriage—"I'll clap you in irons!"

Alexis couldn't help it. She sniggered. *Clap us in irons? Whatever that means.*

"You think this is funny?" asked the deputy. Alexis was about to say no, but they were interrupted by a waitress carrying a paper bag.

"Here's your lunch, *Deputy*," she said with a smile. "Grilled cheese with no crust—just the way you like it." She winked at the girls and handed the officer his bag. . . which had cartoon animals all over it.

Deputy Dewayne saw the girls hide a laugh as they looked from him to the bag.

"The kiddie menu is cheaper!" he exclaimed. "And I *like* it! You just remember what I said. This is my town. Don't get on my bad side!" With that, he turned and

11

marched out of the lobby.

"No way!" said Elizabeth.

"I know!" said Alexis. "Kiddie menu?"

"Clap us in irons?"

Elizabeth shot some pictures of the carriage, and then the girls laughed all the way up the stairs to the room where Alexis's grandmother was giving a speech on British literature. When they reached the door of the room where Mrs. Windsor was teaching, Alexis put a finger to her lips to tell Elizabeth to be quiet.

"And *that*," said Alexis's grandmother's voice, "is how the famous Gunpowder Plot was discovered."

The people applauded lightly and then stood to leave. Alexis had to wait for the group of people around her grandmother to clear before introducing Elizabeth.

"This is my grandma, Molly Windsor."

"It's nice to finally meet you," said the short lady, shaking Elizabeth's hand. Her hair was a powerful shade of red, and her face was covered with a smattering of freckles, just like Alexis's. "I hope you two have been enjoying the scenery!"

"We've only just begun," said Elizabeth. "But we *have* been to the bridge."

Alexis shuddered again.

"Really, Alexis!" said her grandmother. "That

bridge is hardly twenty feet tall and made out of solid concrete and steel! It's perfectly safe. You need to work on that fear of yours!"

"You're afraid of bridges?" cried Elizabeth.

"It's nothing," said Alexis, changing the subject. "Want to go sightseeing with us, Grandma?"

"Sorry, girls. I have two more lectures today. Why don't you explore together? You're bound to find some fascinating things."

She bustled around her podium, taking out another set of notes. Just then, an older man approached the front. Had he been sitting in the back all that time? Or had it just taken him that long to walk up the aisle?

"Interesting topic, Dr. Windsor," he said. His voice sounded like sandpaper under water—scratchy and wet at the same time.

"Thank you," said Alexis's grandmother. "Girls, this is Dr. Edwards. He is speaking this week as well."

The skinny, slouched man reached out to shake hands but pulled back quickly. He yanked a square white piece of fabric out of his front pocket. He held the handkerchief up to his nose and sneezed into it. The violence of the sneeze had not messed up his perfect mustache, which was a glimmering white, like his short hair.

"Forgive me," he said. "The air here is dusty."

"This is my granddaughter, Alexis," said Grandma Windsor. "And her friend Elizabeth. Alexis is staying with me for the week."

The man eyed the girls and frowned.

"Well, hopefully you two will find something better to do than bother the people attending our conference," he said. "The bed race, for example, usually interests the *loud* youth of the city."

"Bed race?" said Alexis. "What's a bed race?" It sounded so interesting that she forgot Dr. Edwards had just insulted them.

"Ask the crazy lady at the front desk," said Dr. Edwards. With that, he bowed to Grandma Windsor and left.

"Don't mind him, girls," said Grandma Windsor when he was out of hearing range. "He's old and grouchy. Gets along better with books than with people."

Another audience began flooding into the room, so Alexis and Elizabeth fought against the tide and left, waving good-bye over their shoulders. They walked back down to the lobby and saw the woman Dr. Edwards had called *the crazy lady* at the front desk.

Of course she wasn't really crazy. She *did* have a streak of purple hair though. Alexis was sure that someone like Dr. Edwards would call that *crazy* instead of *creative, interesting,* or *fun.*

They waited at the desk behind a man who had lost his room key and a woman who needed more towels. When it was their turn, Alexis spoke up.

"Hi," she said. "We're visiting here, and we heard something about a bed race. Could you tell us what that is?"

"Of course!" said the lady. She wasn't old, but she wasn't too young either. The color in her hair made it even harder for Alexis to tell her age. "It's exactly what it sounds like—a bed race!" she said brightly.

Alexis and Elizabeth exchanged a confused look. The lady behind the desk explained further.

"The race happens on Saturday, before the parade. Each team decorates an old bed with wheels on it. Then the teams race the beds through town. Someone pushes or pulls the bed, and the others ride on it. You sign up over *there,*" she pointed to the wall a few feet away. There was a large poster with a picture of a zooming four-poster and a scribbled list of names.

Alexis looked at Elizabeth and could tell she was thinking the same thing: This could be quite the adventure! A cloud passed over Alexis's smile.

"Where are we supposed to get an old bed?" she asked.

"You'd be surprised," said the woman behind the desk. "I'd start looking around the shopping area. Try the older shops—and don't hesitate to ask around."

The girls turned to leave, but the desk lady called out. "I'm Jane, by the way."

"I'm Alexis, and this is Elizabeth."

"Well, good luck! The same team has won two years in a row. Maybe you can show them up, huh?" She waved at the girls and gave them a cheerful smile.

The girls waved back and walked across the lobby toward the front door and the sunshine.

Suddenly the lobby door flew open, and a short, round man with messy gray hair stumbled through it. His face was red beneath a bushy mustache, and sweat poured down his cheeks. Everyone in the area stopped moving and talking. The only sound in the room was the slap of the man's polished shoes as he crossed the marble floor.

"Mr. Mayor, what is it?"

The mayor, thought Alexis. *What could be wrong?*

"Mayor Applebee, can I help?" Jane came out from behind the front desk. The mayor stopped. A bead of sweat flipped off the end of his chin. He raised his hands in the air, as if he were about to make an important announcement.

His breathing was still labored, but it seemed that he couldn't wait any longer. He gulped at the air and spoke.

"The bridge. . .is. . . It's. . ." He almost fell over, but Jane rushed to support him. After a moment the mayor regained his balance. He drew in a breath— more steady this time—and managed to finish a whole sentence.

"The London Bridge is. . .*falling down.*"

Falling Down!

Falling down, falling down.
London Bridge is falling down....

Alexis half expected the mayor to finish the old nursery rhyme.

But there was no "my fair lady." Only a winded man standing in the silence of the lobby and looking distressed. No one spoke, because no one knew what to say. Was this some sort of joke? If so, it wasn't a very good one. No one was laughing.

"The commissioner!" wheezed the mayor. "Where is he?"

"In the restaurant," said Jane. "Eating lunch."

Mayor Applebee took off through the lobby.

"Who is the commissioner?" Alexis asked.

"The bridge commissioner," answered Jane. "He's in charge of the committee that oversees the bridge. Something must really be wrong."

Alexis and Elizabeth followed the flow of people

out of the hotel lobby and toward the canal. A large group was already gathering on the shore, and it was difficult to see the bridge. They could only see a herd of people being shown off the nearest end of the bridge. The food stands that had been selling treats moments earlier were piling everything into boxes. Over the entrance to the bridge, the sign reading TASTES OF HAVASU had been removed, and a police officer was replacing it with yellow caution tape.

There must really be something wrong with the bridge, thought Alexis. "Come on, Elizabeth. Let's see if we can get closer."

The girls edged their way to the front of the crowd and then carefully walked along the water's edge toward the bridge. Eventually they saw it. A crack— about eight feet long—climbing out of the water and reaching toward the arch in the second bridge support. Even as they watched, a bit of mortar crumbled and plunked into the channel.

The crowd gasped.

Voices chimed together, striking chords of worry and fear.

"It couldn't really fall, could it?"

"The middle will go first, if it does."

"I guess that's what happens when you buy a used bridge!"

"What about the parade?"

What about the parade? thought Alexis. She had been so excited about the festival, but could it go on if the bridge was threatening to collapse? Suddenly a voice from the back of the crowd rose above all the others.

"It's the *curse*." The voice was solid but wavy—like an aged piece of oak. The people on the bank all turned. Their eyes locked onto an old woman. She was wearing a ragged brown dress and a cloak, even though it was hot. Her tin-colored hair hung tangled to her waist, and she was leaning on a warped walking stick.

Alexis couldn't tell if it was a costume or not. The lady definitely looked like some kind of medieval hag. The woman reminded her of the old hag in *The Princess Bride*, who cursed Princess Buttercup in her dreams for giving away her own true love.

"What curse?" someone called from the crowd.

"Don't you people keep up on your history?" asked the old woman. She was speaking from the top of the little green hill near the bridge. Everyone could see her as she lifted her hands to speak over them.

"History!" the woman repeated. "The London Bridge never remains whole for long, no matter how you rebuild it. From the time of the Romans, it has always sunk, burned, or *crumbled*!" She pointed toward the crack with her stick.

The crowd began to murmur. Some were nodding. Alexis made a mental note to ask her grandmother about the bridge's destructive past. The old woman continued.

"When the bridge was brought to Lake Havasu, the curse of the River Thames followed. Now it will prey on two cities, instead of one! London and Lake Havasu City are sisters in destruction!"

The people began talking among themselves again. Some wandered back to whatever they had been doing before the commotion. Some called after the woman, asking her questions, but she was already out of reach. She walked toward town singing softly in a croaking voice, *"London Bridge is falling down, falling down, falling down. . . ."*

When the crowd had thinned out, Alexis and Elizabeth wandered closer to the bridge. From the grassy slope they could easily see the crack. It looked strange—harmless and menacing at the same time. Elizabeth sat on the grass and crossed her lanky legs. Alexis plopped down beside her.

"Do you think a crack that small could really bring a whole bridge down?" Elizabeth asked.

"I have no idea!" answered Alexis. "I'm just glad nothing happened while we were up there this morning." Alexis ran her hand through the short grass.

"I just don't get it," she said, picking a small clover. "This bridge shouldn't just fall down. I read about it before I came. The outside layer of stone is from the real London Bridge, but everything underneath is solid steel and cement. It shouldn't be crumbling, Elizabeth."

Alexis was puzzled. What could possibly bring down such a huge structure? The bridge wasn't old— barely thirty years. And it wasn't like Lake Havasu got a lot of severe weather or anything. That only left one possibility.

"The curse," said Alexis, almost in a whisper.

"Alexis, come on," said Elizabeth. Now her gangly arms were crossed as well as her legs. "You can't really believe what that lady was saying. Curses aren't real!"

"I know," said Alexis. "But it sounds like a mystery, don't you think?" She looked sideways at her friend and raised her eyebrows. Elizabeth's mouth stretched into a wide smile.

"Mmm, I was hoping something like this might happen. . . . I mean, not the crack!" she apologized to the bridge. "You know what I mean. Do you happen to have that little pink notebook of yours?"

"What do you think?" said Alexis. She drew the notebook out of her back pocket and started scribbling as Elizabeth listed people they should try to talk to.

Problem: There's a crack in the London Bridge.

Plan: Track down more information. Start by talking to the old woman—maybe there's more to this curse thing than we realize. Maybe it's a stunt for the tourists.

Alexis thought back to the conversation surrounding the bridge only moments before.

"Elizabeth," she said. "What if they cancel the parade? No parade means no bed race! That would be a total bummer!"

"I know," said Elizabeth. "But it's even worse than that. No London Bridge means no Lake Havasu. They built this town around that bridge, Alexis. How many tourists will come to see a pile of rocks?"

"Who knows," said Alexis. "It works for Stonehenge, doesn't it?"

Elizabeth didn't laugh.

"Stonehenge is a pile of big rocks in England that were propped upright sometime way before Jesus was born," Alexis explained, in case Elizabeth didn't know. "They don't know who put them up or why they're standing in a circle in the middle of a field. . . ."

"Oh, I know about that," Elizabeth said. "I saw a program about it on the History Channel. I was just thinking."

"Look!" Alexis whispered. She pointed across the road to where a short, slouched figure was walking quickly away, leaning on a stick. It was the old woman.

"Come on! Let's go talk to her!" Elizabeth exclaimed.

Both girls jumped to their feet and dusted off their backsides before jogging across the street. They wanted to catch up and ask her a few questions about the bridge and this so-called curse, but it wasn't that easy.

The closer they got to the woman, the faster she seemed to walk. Soon she was almost running. She zigged and zagged through the streets of Lake Havasu City, leading the girls deeper and deeper into the teeming crowds of tourists. The old woman took a sharp left into an alley behind a bakery, and the girls almost lost her.

They stood panting on the sidewalk, being jostled by purses. Alexis noticed that some of the purses had small dogs in them. She would never understand what made people carry their dogs around everywhere they went.

"It's like she knows we're following her and is trying to lose us!" panted Elizabeth. "She must be up to something devious, or she wouldn't run."

"I know," wheezed Alexis as a Pomeranian nipped at her elbow from inside its rainbow-colored Louis Vuitton. "Can you see anything?"

Elizabeth used her height to peer over the heads of the crowd.

"There!" she cried. The old woman emerged from an alley farther down the street. She bent low, as if she didn't want to be seen.

The girls resumed the chase.

"Maybe she's late for an appointment," said Alexis, fighting against the pressure of bodies as they weaved through yet another crosswalk. At that moment the woman turned around. The girls emerged from a clump of people, and they made eye contact.

The woman ran.

Now Alexis knew that the woman was definitely avoiding them. But why? It didn't make any sense. She was the one who had stood near the bridge yelling about a curse. All they wanted was a little more information, for goodness' sake! And for a rickety, old-looking woman, she sure ran fast!

They ran for half a mile or more, making three

left-hand turns and four to the right. Then Elizabeth stopped.

"She's gone," she huffed.

"Are you sure?" asked Alexis.

"Sure." Elizabeth bent over to catch her breath. "I haven't seen her for a few minutes. She got away."

Alexis slumped against the nearest window. It was cold to the touch. The store must have had the air-conditioning going full blast. *Well*, she thought, *there's nothing left to do now but go back.* She looked around. . . and recognized nothing.

"Elizabeth, do you know where we are?"

Her friend only shook her head. Great. They were alone in a strange city, and they had followed the old woman without even thinking about how they would get back. Alexis thought of *Hansel and Gretel.*

"Those two were smart," she said.

"What?" asked Elizabeth.

"Hansel and Gretel were smart. They left a way to get back home."

Elizabeth laughed. "Sure. I'll keep a few bread crumbs in my pocket for our next high-speed chase through a strange town!"

"I guess we can go in a shop and ask someone," said Alexis.

Elizabeth was about to answer when they both jumped.

Hundreds of screams ripped through the streets of Lake Havasu City.

CHAPTER 3

Imposters

The air was quiet for a moment or two. Then it happened again. Hundreds of people screamed.

Alexis looked at Elizabeth. By the fear on her friend's face she could tell that Elizabeth was also worried. They were two young girls alone in a strange place. Frantic screams filled the air. They did the only thing two Camp Club Girls would have done. They ran. . .toward the screaming.

When they rounded the last corner, the screaming finally made sense. Alexis and Elizabeth stood facing a huge building. Glittering letters on the side of it told them it was Lake Havasu High School, home of the Fighting Knights. The noise was coming from inside the gym. A few straggling students made their way through a pair of double doors.

"Look, Alexis." Elizabeth pointed to another sign. It was splashed bright with purple and gold poster paint: PEP RALLY TODAY! GO KNIGHTS!

"Want to take a look?" asked Alexis. She had been to one pep rally at her middle school, but it had been pretty lame. It hadn't been for a sport or anything. Just an assembly meant to encourage the students to do their best in school this year. Who had ever heard of a "Yay for Homework!" rally?

Alexis had never even been inside a high school. How cool would it be to tell her friends she'd seen a high school pep rally, even if it was from the outside?

The girls edged toward the doors, trying to get a peek before they closed. A voice behind them made them jump.

"Hey! Get in there, or you'll miss it!"

The man ordering them into the building was obviously a teacher. Elizabeth tried to explain that they were tourists, but the man held up a thick, pink pad of paper.

"Please," he said. "Don't make me give out two more detentions."

At that point the girls figured it was useless to protest. He lightly nudged them through the doors, followed them in, and closed the doors with a snap.

Immediately the girls' senses were overloaded.

The horns of the marching band wailed what must have been the school song. The rhythm of the drums was constant and violent, like the heartbeat of an enormous beast. The bleachers exploded with a chant, "Go, Knights, go! Fight, Knights, fight! Go! Fight! *WIN!*" Then more of the screaming the girls had heard from the street.

Alexis didn't know whether to be afraid of high school or extremely excited to be a part of it. Just then she saw something that made up her mind. Five of the cheerleaders, dazzling in purple and gold, gathered in a small clump. The girl in the center disappeared for a moment, and someone yelled, "One, two!"

The cheerleaders moved down together, and when they rose, the tiny girl in the middle exploded toward the ceiling. She completed a backflip before slamming her hands out to meet her toes and falling gracefully back into her teammates' waiting arms.

Alexis's mouth hung open in shock. She had never seen a stunt go that high. Sometimes the girls throwing her in practice barely got her above their heads. She was sure this cheerleader had almost hit the rafters of the looming gym. And she knew that she was going to fly like that one day. No matter what it took.

Someone nudged her. It was the teacher again. He pointed over to the bleachers labeled FRESHMEN, and Alexis and Elizabeth squeezed into the front row.

"Hey, you don't go to school here." The voice came from a blond boy next to Elizabeth. It wasn't accusing, just amused. "I've never seen you before. You're imposters! I would have noticed you," he added, winking at Elizabeth. The girls ignored him.

A tall girl with purple face paint walked to the center of the gym. She was holding a microphone.

"Attention, Fighting Knights! It's time for the class competition! Now we're going to pick one member from each class. Who will win? The freshmen? Sophomores? Juniors? Or seniors?"

The students roared, and before Alexis realized what was going on, the blond boy had shoved her from her spot on the bench.

"Alrighty! I have a freshman volunteer," the tall girl said, grabbing Alexis by the hand.

Alexis looked at Elizabeth frantically, but Elizabeth just shrugged in a hopeless "What can I do?" expression.

The tall girl with the purple face dragged Alexis onto the hardwood. Alexis stood in front of a thousand teenagers, petrified.

Didn't they know she didn't belong here? Surely it was painted on her like one of their posters. The blond boy had known right away.

Whether or not they knew, nobody said anything. Three older students joined her in the middle of the floor: one sophomore, one junior, and one senior. Cheerleaders pulled two red wagons into the middle of the floor.

"Here, you two work together," the tall girl commanded as she placed Alexis next to the sophomore—a short, chunky boy with glasses. The girl holding the microphone gave Alexis a broomstick and then spoke to the crowd.

"Since this week is the London Bridge Festival, our competition today is the wagon joust!" The gym erupted. "Each team will have two chances to collect as many rings on their broomsticks as possible. As always, seniors and juniors first!"

The other team got ready. One got in the wagon with the broomstick, and the other got ready to pull. Small hula hoops hung from fishing string down the middle of the gym. The person with the broom was supposed to grab them by passing the broom through the middle as they raced past.

All at once, the wagon took off. It was more than a little bit wobbly. The person pulling the wagon had a hard time steering, and the team missed the first three hoops because they weren't close enough.

They weaved some and grabbed two hoops before getting tangled in the third and tumbling over. The students in the gym laughed as the competitors got up and tried their second run. They got three more hoops, giving them a total of five. The older students roared their approval and booed as Alexis climbed in her wagon.

"That's probably a good idea that they gave you the broom," her partner said with a laugh. "I don't think I would fit in that wagon! And if I could, I don't think you'd be able to pull me!"

"Just keep us going straight, okay?" said Alexis. She took a deep breath. How on earth had she gotten herself into this?

They were off. The boy was pulling Alexis a lot faster than she had expected to go. How long had it been since she had been in a wagon anyway? No time to think about it. The first hoop tore by before she realized it, but the next three slid easily onto the end of her stick.

Cheers erupted from the younger side of the gym.

When she picked up a fourth hoop, the broomstick got heavy, and it slipped off before she could lift the handle. They reached the end of the gym and turned around. Alexis only needed to get three more hoops to win.

They tore back down the way they had come, and Alexis aimed for the three hoops left behind. Two slid on easily, but the third spun round and round on the handle, threatening to fly into the audience. The wagon stopped suddenly, and Alexis flew out.

The crowd gasped.

Alexis was lying on her back. She lifted her broomstick in the air, and the girl with the microphone counted out loud.

"Six!" she cried. "The freshmen and sophomores win, probably for the first time in ten years!"

The boos of the older students were drowned out by the higher-pitched cheers of the freshmen and sophomores. Alexis scooted back to her seat, blushing like crazy.

"Alexis, you're amazing!" said Elizabeth.

"Thanks," said Alexis. She elbowed her way in next to the blond boy. "Thanks to you, too," she said, pushing him playfully.

"It wasn't that bad, was it?" He laughed.

The microphone girl called for silence.

"Now," she said, "it's time for the reason we're all here in the first place! Let's give it up for your Lake Havasu High School swim team!"

Again the crowd went wild.

"The swim team?" said Alexis and Elizabeth together. Elizabeth leaned over Alexis and addressed the blond boy.

"Aren't pep rallies usually for football or something? I've never heard of a pep rally for the swim team."

"I know," replied the blond boy. "This is the first time the school has had a pep rally for the swim team. But this is more for one guy than the whole team. You see those?" He pointed up to the gym ceiling, and Alexis noticed a collection of banners for the first time. They were purple satin lined with gold. Each one had STATE CHAMPION embroidered along the top with a different event underneath. *100 m Butterfly, 100 m Freestyle, 400 m Individual Medley.* All six of them were labeled with the same name: *David Turner.*

"That's him," said the blond boy. He pointed across the gym to where one member of the swim team stood a little behind the others. "He's only a freshman, too. He won all of those last year, before he was even in high school. The guy's a machine. So they decided that the swim team is worthy of being honored this year with a pep rally."

"Wow," said Elizabeth. Alexis was speechless. Something about the swim champion bothered her. Everyone in the school was clapping and screaming for *him*, but he didn't seem to like it. He was off to the side, the hood of his sweatshirt pulled in front of his face and his lanky shoulders stooped. Alexis got the feeling that he wished he were invisible.

The coach who was with the team grabbed a microphone and announced that the team would have a swim meet the following afternoon. It would be held at four o'clock at the Aquatic Center in town.

From the noise and excitement of the screaming crowd, Alexis guessed that just about everyone would be there. She thought it was kind of funny. She wondered if the schools in her area even *had* swim teams. She made a mental note to check when she got back to Sacramento.

The gym began to empty, and students filed out of the gym to go back to their classes. Alexis and Elizabeth slipped out the door to the street, making sure to avoid the teacher who had led them inside. They walked back the way they had come.

Soon they were melting in the heat. A sign up ahead rocked in the breeze. It had a triple-scoop ice cream cone on it.

"What do you think?" asked Alexis. "We can ask for directions to the hotel and get a snack at the same time."

"Perfect!" said Elizabeth.

The girls walked into the shop and sighed with delight as the cool of the air-conditioning mingled with the warm smell of fresh waffle cones. Alexis ordered a scoop of chocolate and a scoop of rainbow sherbet.

"Those don't go together!" said Elizabeth.

"Of course they do!" said Alexis. "What am I supposed to do when I can't decide between chocolate or fruity?"

The girls sat in a squishy booth near the front window and watched the tourists amble by. Their conversation shifted back to the Lake Havasu swim champion.

"I can't believe that!" said Alexis. "He must be really good to have won all of those championships."

"I know!" said Elizabeth. "And he beat a bunch of older swimmers to get them!"

The bell on the ice cream shop door jingled.

The mayor walked through the door and up to the counter, followed by the bridge commissioner and a crumpled old man sniffling into a hankie. Alexis choked on a bite of her rainbow sherbet.

"Elizabeth, look! What is Dr. Edwards doing with Mayor Applebee and the bridge commissioner?"

"Shh!" said Elizabeth. She motioned to Alexis, and the girls slumped down in their booth. The three men sat in the next booth over.

"You sure you don't want anything, Dr. Edwards?" asked the mayor. The only answer was another sneeze. "I suggested the ice cream shop just to get out of the office," continued the mayor. "All I've heard about all day is that silly curse. My phone has been ringing off the hook!"

"I can assure you, Mayor," said Dr. Edwards, "there is no such thing as the curse of the Thames. History never mentions it. It's just a story someone has made up to scare the tourists."

A deeper, calmer voice broke into the conversation. Alexis knew it had to be the bridge commissioner.

"Curse or not, something's wrong with our bridge. The engineers are flying in tomorrow. If there is any structural damage, the parade can't happen."

"Aren't you being hasty, Commissioner?" said Dr. Edwards.

"Are you trying to tell me how to do my job, Doctor?"

"Gentlemen, gentlemen," said the mayor. "Let's get along, shall we?"

"We can't let years of tradition be stopped by a tiny crack!" Dr. Edwards pounded the table.

"Have you ever seen an avalanche, Doctor?" asked the commissioner. "It all starts with a tiny crack, and then. . .*boom!* Everything goes down, and there's no stopping it.

"To take a chance on the parade would be totally foolhardy. Can you imagine the bridge collapsing with dozens or even hundreds of people on it? Imagine the injuries and even deaths."

"But the chances of that are probably slim," Dr. Edwards said, his voice rising. "If we have to cancel the parade this year, many people probably won't return next year. Our tradition will be lost. *That* would be foolhardy!"

"Yes," said the commissioner. "And imagine how many people will never return and what will happen to the tradition if a tragedy should happen."

"Alright, alright!" said Mayor Applebee. "No more fighting! We all want the parade to go on as planned, but safety must come first. If the bridge is okay, it will happen. If something is wrong. . ." He sighed heavily and stood up, carrying the last of his now dripping ice cream cone. The other two men followed him out of the shop, still arguing.

"Why is Dr. Edwards so concerned about the parade?" asked Elizabeth.

"I have no idea," said Alexis. It didn't make sense. "The mayor might have asked him about the curse, since the doctor is an expert in English history. But why did Dr. Edwards get so angry about the idea of canceling the parade?"

"I wouldn't have thought Dr. Edwards was the type of person who would even enjoy a parade," said Elizabeth. "Actually, I can't imagine him enjoying *anything*."

"That's what I was just thinking," Alexis said.

"Well," said Elizabeth, "do you want to walk back to the hotel? We could hit the pool and go swimming before dinner."

"Sounds good," said Alexis. They got directions and walked the streets silently. Alexis was still trying to figure out why Dr. Edwards cared so much about the problem with the bridge. It sounded like the bridge commissioner was pretty worried. Alexis couldn't stop thinking about one thing he had said. *"It all starts with a tiny crack, and then. . .boom!"*

The more Alexis thought about it, the more she realized the commissioner was right. But not just about the bridge. Sometimes the smallest things could cause the biggest problems. Like this summer, for instance. Her friend Jerry had wanted to help

Miss Maria save her nature park in Sacramento. Her business had dropped, and she'd brought in mechanical dinosaurs. But what Jerry had thought was harmless fun ended up as a huge news story and a mystery for the Camp Club Girls to solve. But feelings had gotten hurt, and Miss Maria even got injured because of Jerry's little idea.

"Elizabeth," said Alexis. "Isn't there something in the Bible about small things causing big problems?"

"Well, there are a few things," said Elizabeth. "A verse or two talks about little foxes spoiling the vineyards, which means small things that we tend to ignore can bring destruction. And in the book of James, we're told that our tongue, even though it's so small, can do big-time damage."

Alexis and Elizabeth walked in silence for a few minutes. Then Alexis suddenly turned to Elizabeth.

"What did you say?" she asked.

"Huh?"

"I thought you said something," said Alexis. She looked around. Not too many people were outside now since it was the hottest time of the day. They were near the alley where they had lost the old woman earlier. Alexis strained her ears and heard it again—a hurried whisper.

She edged toward the alley but didn't look around the corner. The words were muffled, but she heard them loud and clear.

"We have to steal the whole carriage."

A second voice began to argue.

"How are we gonna get it out of the hotel?"

The hotel? Alexis thought. Were these people seriously talking about stealing the golden carriage from the London Bridge Resort?

Elizabeth let out a quiet gasp, and the girls looked at each other.

"Don't worry," said the first voice again. "It'll be easy. And smile—this job is worth millions."

CHAPTER 4

The Golden Coach

Suddenly Alexis heard rustling, as if the people who had been speaking were moving toward them.

Elizabeth grabbed her arm and motioned for them to leave.

Alexis hated to go without at least getting a look at the whisperers. But the rustling seemed to draw closer.

The girls fled. They didn't know what else to do. What would happen if the people in the alley knew Alexis and Elizabeth had heard their plan?

They had run close to two miles when they finally saw the London Bridge Resort. Alexis was grateful to see its towers.

This must have been how retreating armies felt once they had left the danger of the battlefield and found the safety of their castle walls again, she thought.

Alexis and Elizabeth stood in the lobby, panting and trying to catch their breath. Their eyes were drawn toward the carriage. It was absolutely huge. Could anyone really think they would be able to steal this thing?

Alexis walked over to a sign standing near the ropes protecting the golden masterpiece. It gave a brief history of the original carriage and the replica.

The Golden State Coach was built in London in 1762. King George III commissioned it and meant to ride in it on the day of his coronation. The greatness of the coach, however, kept it from being finished until three years later. Nonetheless, King George III and his family used it as the Coach of State. Recent monarchs have used the coach once a year in their customary parade to open Parliament. The last time the coach was used was by Elizabeth II in 2002.

This priceless replica is the only full-size model of the original coach. It was built for the use of the London Bridge Resort and Hotel.

Alexis looked around the hotel lobby. It was filled with people. Tourists were on their way to dinner. Bellhops ran for the elevators with teetering piles of suitcases. Jane, with her purple hair, was busily checking people in and getting fresh towels or extra pillows.

Alexis knew she wouldn't be able to get near the carriage unnoticed. If she tried, she probably wouldn't make it over the ropes before someone yanked her out.

How did anyone expect to *remove* the carriage from the room entirely? It just didn't seem possible.

Alexis felt a bony elbow digging into her side. She looked up at Elizabeth, who pointed across the carriage to a row of red velvet chairs. Dr. Edwards sat in one, not seeming to even be aware of the hustle and bustle all around him. His head was bowed over a notebook in his lap. His arched hands supported his forehead.

Curious, the girls watched him. Within a few minutes he shook off his daze, stood up hastily, and dashed out of the lobby more quickly than the girls thought he was even capable of moving.

A piece of paper fluttered out of his notebook and onto the floor.

The girls ran over and picked it up.

"Dr. Edwards!" called Alexis. "You dropped something!"

But the man was already in an elevator, and he didn't hear her. Alexis glanced at the paper in her hand, and her eyes opened wide. The paper was thick and unlined with frayed holes along one side, like it had been torn from a sketchbook. On it was a perfect pencil sketch of the Golden State Coach.

"Man," said Elizabeth. "He's a pretty good artist.

Look, he even drew the swirly detail on the dolphin's tail! What's that writing say?" She pointed to the bottom corner where a sentence was scrawled. Alexis pulled the paper closer to her face. She had assumed the writing was just the artist's name or something, but it wasn't. It was a question, written in perfect cursive.

Where could it be hiding?

"Where could it be hiding? That doesn't make any sense," Alexis said.

"The carriage isn't hiding at all. It's in plain sight," Elizabeth added. "So what does that mean?"

"I don't know," Alexis said. "I think maybe we'll have to think about it. For right now I'll put this in my notebook. Do you have your computer here?"

"My dad has his MacBook. I can use that," Elizabeth said.

"Good. I don't have a notebook computer, and Grandma's practically in the Dark Ages—she only has a big old desktop back home," Alexis said. "Why don't you go online tonight and set Kate or Sydney busy seeing if they can find anything about the coach being in hiding."

"Will do," Elizabeth said.

"I think we also need more background information than we have," Alexis said. "The sign was helpful, but we need more."

"I can ask the girls to dig up everything they can on the coach," Elizabeth said.

Alexis grinned at her. "You forget that we have an expert right here. I'll ask Grandma about it tonight while you're filling the girls in. There isn't much about English history that she doesn't know. And I know she brushed up on the carriage and everything pertaining to the London Bridge before she came here."

"Perfect," said Elizabeth. "It's about time for me to get back for dinner anyway. See you tomorrow?"

"Definitely. We'll have a lot to look into. Maybe we'll have time to see the swim meet between investigations." Alexis smiled. Why was she so interested in swimming all of a sudden? It must have been the pep rally.

Elizabeth hugged her and left the hotel.

Alexis stood in the crowded lobby waiting for an elevator to take her to the top floor, where her grandmother and she were sharing a suite. Their suite was amazing. It had two bedrooms with king-size beds, a dining room, a living room with a big-screen TV, and its own kitchen. They didn't really use the kitchen, except to store some drinks in the fridge. Most meals they got for free from the hotel—another one of Grandma Windsor's perks.

Alexis entered the room and saw piles of food on the small table in the living room. Grandma Windsor was on the couch, already in her pajamas and fluffy slippers.

"I thought we'd do room service tonight!" she called through a mouth full of pizza. Alexis laughed, imagining what her mom would say if she spoke with her mouth full, like Grandma Windsor had.

"Perfect!" said Alexis. She changed into boxer shorts and a tank top and plopped down next to her grandma in front of the TV. They watched a bit of the news, and Alexis saw that Elizabeth's dad had caught the largest fish in the first day of the bass tournament. She was surprised to see no news of the bridge. She guessed the mayor was keeping everything quiet until they found out what was going on.

After the pizza was gone, Alexis popped open a Mountain Dew and got comfy.

"So, that coach thing downstairs is pretty cool," she said, acting just a little bit interested. For some reason she didn't want to come right out and say, "Someone's trying to steal the coach!" She didn't have any evidence besides a whispered conversation in an alley. And what if the people had only been joking?

"Yes," said Grandma Windsor, "the coach is an amazing replica. The real one was part of a very historical reign in England."

"You mean King George the Third?" asked Alexis, remembering the name from the sign in the lobby.

"Yes, Alexis! I'm proud of you!" Grandma Windsor muted the TV, excited to talk about her favorite subject. "King George the Third was famous for two things, mostly."

"What were they?" asked Alexis.

"Losing the American Revolutionary War and going crazy."

"He went crazy?" Alexis had never enjoyed history class, but for some reason she loved it when her grandmother told her stories like this. The characters seemed so much more real than the ones in her schoolbooks.

"Well, yes," said her grandma. "That's what they say. It may have been the pressure, of course. Being a king isn't easy. Scholars today, however, believe that he was probably genetically predisposed to mental illness and that he had a blood disease."

"What?" asked Alexis.

"It means that his mind might have always been a little fragile. He might have always been mentally unbalanced. If he had been in charge of the country while it was peaceful and wealthy, maybe he wouldn't have snapped. But he didn't live during peace, and he *did* finally snap." Grandma Windsor clicked the TV off.

"How did people know he was crazy?" asked Alexis. She felt sad for this king who had collapsed under the weight of his crown.

"Well, he didn't really lose his mind until his later years. They say it happened after his youngest daughter died. Her name was Princess Amelia, and she was his favorite. In fact, the king was so protective of his daughters that he didn't want them to marry. There were rumors that the young Amelia had fallen in love with someone below her rank. A princess would never be allowed to marry a horse trainer."

"That's awful!" said Alexis. She imagined a beautiful young princess locked in a tower, while her crazy father kept the key on a chain around his neck. The wonderful and extremely handsome boy who wanted to marry the princess stood beneath the tower, day and night, waiting.

Alexis was becoming what her mother called a "romantic type" of person.

Alexis forgot about the mystery surrounding the carriage as Grandma Windsor told story after story about crazy King George III. Alexis learned that Princess Amelia had sent secret letters to the one she loved. Then she had become ill and died without ever getting married.

Alexis asked what happened to the letters, but her grandmother didn't know.

When Alexis and her grandmother stopped talking, she called Elizabeth and passed along what she'd learned.

"The girls all said to tell you hi," Elizabeth said. "McKenzie thought it was a rip-off that you had to ride a wagon instead of a real horse to joust today. Sydney wanted more information on the swimming team since she's so into sports. Kate wishes she would have sent you a prototype her dad has of a new iPad clone so we could keep them posted every minute. Kate is going to look up information. She said any time we have news to text her and she'll circulate it to the rest of the girls.

"Bailey is really proud of you for winning the contest in the school today. She wants to know if either of us are going to try to be the pageant queen. And dear little Biscuit the Wonder Dog even woofed. I think he was saying if he'd been with us today he would have caught the old hag for us!"

Alexis laughed. The messages sounded so much

like the Camp Club Girls! Count on the Camp Club Girls to be there with them in spirit, in thought, and in prayers!

"Can you text Kate and ask her to check into letters Grandma mentioned that were written by Princess Amelia?" Alexis asked.

"Sure," Elizabeth replied. "I think I'll also ask her to check into curses surrounding the London Bridge."

With that, the girls said good night.

When Alexis finally climbed into bed, her mind was swimming with pictures of royalty: beautiful gowns, golden coaches, and lost letters of love. Eventually she fell asleep to the sound of water slapping the bridge outside her window.

And she dreamed.

She was walking along the London Bridge again, only this time she was not afraid. Halfway across she stopped to look over the rail. The reflection of the full moon sparkled brightly in the night, rippling with the small waves. Suddenly she heard a voice. A sweet voice, singing a familiar tune.

"London Bridge is falling down, falling down, falling down. . . ."

It was a girl not much older than Alexis—maybe fifteen or sixteen. Her dress looked old-fashioned but gorgeous. Silver silk sparkling in the starlight. Pearls were strung throughout her long waves of dark hair. They matched the necklace around her delicate throat. The girl's liquid eyes didn't see Alexis, but she stopped to look over the rail, too, farther down the bridge.

The young girl took something from the inside of her gown—a folded piece of paper. She hugged it to her chest. Then she kissed it and let it drift down into the lake. She turned away and kept walking toward the other side of the bridge. She kept singing.

"London Bridge is falling down, my fair lady."

The bridge rumbled. The girl disappeared as a thick fog rolled up from the water to engulf everything. Her sweet voice vanished as well and was replaced by an older voice.

"My fair lady!" It shrieked, and then it laughed. The long, dry cackle was all too familiar. It was the voice of the old crone Elizabeth and Alexis had seen earlier in the day. Alexis could see the outline of a bent form through the fog. The figure lifted a walking stick high into the air and brought it down hard onto the stonework of the bridge.

The bridge rumbled again, and this time it rocked. The rail in front of Alexis broke away and fell toward the water. . .and she followed it.

Alexis wanted to scream, but her voice was caught in her throat. Stone and cement surrounded her as she plummeted into the water. It was icy, and the stabbing cold stole her breath. She fought to swim, every moment expecting a piece of the London Bridge to crush her and push her to the bottom.

A few feet away something white was floating on the surface. It was the girl's letter, and it was soaked through. With what? *Alexis wondered. Tears or water?*

One more breath, that's all she could take. Her arms hurt. They couldn't support her anymore. She was sinking.

An arm. A long, thin arm reached out and grabbed her. Alexis was pulled to the safety of the shore by the powerful sidestroke of a swimming prince.

The Message of the Moon

The next morning, Alexis met Elizabeth outside her hotel. There were loud voices coming from the area of the bridge, so naturally they drifted in that direction. When the bridge came into view, Alexis's dream came flooding back. She shuddered.

She almost told Elizabeth about it but decided not to. It had really been weird, and she didn't think she could remember it all anyway.

"Look," said Elizabeth. "The bridge is still closed."

The bridge looked different than it had the day before. It was still decorated with yellow caution tape, but now there were big men in hard hats crawling all over it. They were all using strange instruments that looked like levels. A few of them were even in the water near the closest pillar. It was only up to their waist.

"That's funny," said Alexis. "I thought the water was a lot deeper than that."

"Those must be the engineers," said Elizabeth.

"Good. It shouldn't take them long to figure out what's going on." Alexis led Elizabeth farther down the grassy slope, and they sat on the little beach, about twenty feet from the yellow tape. "Hopefully the festival can pick up where it left off."

The men in the water were pointing toward the second pillar, where the crack had grown overnight. They seemed to be arguing about something.

"That's strange," said Elizabeth.

"What?" asked Alexis.

"The crack. It's reaching *up* the arch of the bridge. See? It's climbing closer to the top every day."

"I know," said Alexis. "That means whatever is causing the crack is under the water."

"I wonder what it could be," said Elizabeth. She shot Alexis a sneaky look. "We could check it out, you know."

"What? You mean under the water?" Alexis's heart began to pound. Not only was she afraid of bridges, but last night she had also dreamed of this particular bridge falling on top of her. "That's crazy! The engineers aren't even getting close to that crack!"

"It's not crazy," said Elizabeth. She leaned forward and shielded her eyes from the sun. She squinted, looking toward the middle of the river where the crack loomed. "The channel under the bridge is only eight feet deep in the middle. A lady at my hotel told me."

"Okay," said Alexis. "Keep in mind that I am barely five feet tall. You, my giant friend, may be able to tiptoe out there, but I. . ." Alexis shivered again. Her dream had been way too realistic.

"Oh come on, Alexis! All we need is a couple pairs of goggles. We brought our swimsuits, right? We can walk out most of the way, swim the last few feet to the pillar, and dunk our heads under to check out the crack."

Alexis was just about to say, "I'll think about it," when a noise behind them made them jump. Chipper whistling. . .to the tune of "London Bridge."

The girls spun around where they sat and saw the old woman dressed as a hag coming toward the bridge. She spotted them, but she didn't run away this time. Instead she turned a little so she was heading right for them. The spring in her step told Alexis the old lady was in a good mood and that maybe she wasn't as old as they had thought. She kept whistling as she reached the bench near the sidewalk. Alexis moved to get up, but a sharp whistle made her freeze.

She looked up, and the old woman raised her

eyebrows and shook a finger at her. Then she sat on the bench and looked around, much like a tourist just enjoying the view. *What in the world is going on?* thought Alexis. She watched the woman for almost five minutes before anything else happened.

The lady reached into the pocket of her ragged robe and drew out a small, yellow envelope. She held it in front of her for a moment and looked at the girls to make sure they saw it. Then she placed it beside her on the bench, got up, and left—whistling her tune again.

Alexis and Elizabeth looked at each other. They both asked the same question.

"What was that all about?"

When they could no longer see or hear the old woman, Alexis got up and approached the bench. The little yellow envelope lay facedown on the seat. Alexis picked it up and flipped it over. Three words were scratched on the front:

For the Curious

Alexis looked at Elizabeth and shrugged her shoulders. She tore the envelope open and pulled out a matching note card. The twiglike handwriting said:

442 Lakeview Avenue
7:00 tonight. Don't be late.

That was all. No name. Nothing.

The girls exchanged glances again. What on earth did this mean?

"I guess she wants to talk to us," said Elizabeth.

"Yeah," said Alexis. "But why tonight? At. . .four hundred and forty-two Lakeview Avenue? Why not here and now? Wouldn't that have been more convenient?"

"Maybe," said Elizabeth. "But maybe there's more to it. Maybe she wants to talk where no one can overhear."

They glanced over their shoulders to where the engineers were still investigating the bridge.

"Or," said Alexis, "maybe she wants to lock us in a cage, fatten us up, and throw us into her giant oven."

"Enough with the *Hansel and Gretel* stuff, okay?" said Elizabeth. "Do you want to investigate this stuff or not?"

"Of course I do!" said Alexis. "I think my imagination keeps running away with me." Alexis had no idea why she had been so freaked out lately. Maybe the dream and the bridge had her on edge. Whatever it was, she needed to get over it. She had never thought of herself as a chicken before.

"It's okay, Alex," said Elizabeth. "It's easy to let that happen here. Half the town thinks it's back in seventeenth-century London. You know what you need?"

"Huh?"

"A little water to wake you up."

Alexis took a fearful step back and pointed to the channel. "I'm not going in there."

"Not the lake, nerd! The swim meet! It will give us something to do until we go meet Miss Creepy."

Alexis lit up. "Yes! Let's go!"

Again she asked herself the question: Why was she so excited about a swim meet? Maybe it was just the allure of something new. She'd never been to one before.

The girls walked across downtown to the Aquatic Center. Alexis thought it looked like a giant concrete ice cube. They were greeted by more purple and gold signs and a gaggle of giggling girls. It looked like the entire female population of Lake Havasu City had shown up.

Other schools were there, too. Alexis could tell by the many different colors on the swimming caps of the swimmers. Yellow and black, green and silver, red and blue—just like her school colors back home.

She and Elizabeth found seats halfway up the bleachers. From this place they could see everything. Swimmers were warming up or cooling down in a smaller pool at one end. The huge pool in the middle was divided into eight lanes. Small platforms lined one end.

Within minutes the crowd was on its feet screaming. Alexis and Elizabeth stood, too, so they could see. A woman with huge hair was standing right in front of Alexis. Elizabeth looked over and laughed.

"Here," she said. "Trade me spots!" The girls swapped seats, and Alexis saw the reason for the insanity. The Arizona swimming champion was making his way to one of the platforms at the edge of the pool.

"In lane five," said an intercom voice over the crowd, "David Turner!"

The crowd roared. All the other swimmers had waved and smiled up at the crowd when their names were called. Turner kept his eyes on the water in front of him. The swimmers bent forward, ready to enter the water, and the gun went off.

One swimmer on the end had been late jumping off, but everyone else was already gone. In the middle of the pool Turner hadn't yet broken the surface. He powered through the water, moving his body like a dolphin, until he was almost halfway across. Then his arms came up at the same time, propelling his head and shoulders out of the water as they pushed back under.

It looked as if he were flying.

"So *that's* why they call it the butterfly," said Alexis. She had always heard of the butterfly stroke but had never seen what it looked like.

Turner was at the end of the pool, diving underwater to turn around. When he finished, the person in second place was still in the middle of the pool. The crowd cheered. Turner didn't even look up at the board that showed the swimmers' times in bright lights.

The crowd settled a little as the other swimmers filed out of the pool. The other competitors were greeted by warm hugs of family and the excited smiles of friends. Alexis saw David Turner receive a wet slap on the back from his coach before he slipped away to the locker room. Alone.

His fans, who were still cheering for him, hadn't even noticed he was gone.

"He always looks so sad," said Alexis out loud.

"What?" said Elizabeth, who was watching another race that had already started.

"Nothing," said Alexis. But she couldn't help thinking about the champion. How could someone be so popular—so adored—and still look so alone?

— • —

The girls watched the rest of the meet and then went to meet Elizabeth's family for dinner. They ate at a little café near the square, where the jousting tournament was taking place. The sound of clashing metal and pounding hooves made it easy to ignore Elizabeth's little brother, who kept pretending to pick his nose.

"Talk about little things that spoil stuff," Elizabeth said to Alexis, nodding at her brother. "He's a case in point!"

Alexis's reply was drowned out by the thud of hooves. Every few minutes gigantic horses charged each other. The men on their backs wore real armor and held shields and lances.

Alexis was about to ask why they had to wear the armor when two knights clashed. The lance that the blue knight was holding slammed into the green knight's shield, snapped in half, and then slid up and landed with a crack on the piece of metal protecting the man's throat.

That was why they were wearing real armor.

"Hey, this isn't any game!" she exclaimed to Elizabeth.

"What, jousting?" Elizabeth asked.

"Yes, I guess I thought they were like stuntmen. I

didn't realize they were really fighting," she said.

"Jousting is a big hobby all over the United States," Elizabeth said. "A lot of regions have jousting clubs where they're really into it. A lot of cities have Renaissance festivals where jousting is part of the action."

"Do people often get hurt?" Alexis asked.

"I don't know," Elizabeth admitted. "I guess they sometimes have accidents, but I haven't really paid attention or heard much about it."

Alexis had no idea that people still did this kind of thing. Her heart was beating so fast she could hardly eat.

After dinner the girls began wandering through the streets of downtown. Alexis had gotten a map at her hotel that showed them how to get to 442 Lakeview Avenue. They followed the tiny red lines that indicated where streets were block after block. Finally they ended up in a small neighborhood.

The houses were perfect. Each one was small and built of stone or brick. Short fences surrounded each front yard, and wild—but beautiful—English gardens were in full bloom. The fall flowers filled the air with a smell that reminded Alexis of the honeysuckle back home in Sacramento.

When they finally reached number 442, it was getting dark.

"It doesn't look like anyone is home," said Elizabeth.

The girls walked up to the porch, and sure enough, no lights were on inside the house. The flicker of a light with an electrical short licked at the darkness, throwing shadows against the front door.

"Maybe she forgot," said Alexis. "Let's take a look around to be sure she's not home."

Elizabeth knocked, and Alexis left the porch to peek into the first window. The other side was absolute darkness. There was no way to tell what was inside. That didn't matter, really, but Alexis found that she was very interested to see how this woman lived.

"Do you think this woman is really creepy, or is she pretending?" she asked Elizabeth.

"I don't know," Elizabeth said. "Does she dress up and walk around town cackling to entertain the tourists? Or is there more to her?"

"It's awfully dark around here," Alexis said. "Reminds me of a scary movie."

"'Men loved darkness instead of light because their deeds were evil,'" Elizabeth quoted. "John 3:19. Sometimes the Bible just has the perfect words!"

"I don't think anyone is home," Elizabeth added.

"Yeah, maybe we'd better leave," Alexis said. "It's too much like a scary movie."

"Yep. It's after dark. Two young girls out alone. Supposed to meet someone at a house, but the house is empty," Elizabeth said.

"And the light is flickering," Alexis added.

"Now all we need is—" She abruptly stopped talking as the girls heard footsteps.

They heard the footsteps turn off the sidewalk and enter the gate of 442 Lakeview Avenue. The girls spun around, expecting to see the old woman. Instead, a tall man raised something over his head. It looked like a short baseball bat.

He was coming toward them!

Alexis tried to scream. Elizabeth covered her head.

Then the object in the man's hand blinded them.

It was a flashlight.

"What are you doing poking around people's houses?"

"Oh no," groaned Alexis. It was Deputy Dewayne, the officer the girls had met on their first day in Lake Havasu City.

"I got a call about some trespassers, so I came to *investigate*."

"We're not poking, really, sir," said Alexis. "We had an appointment. We were supposed to come see this woman at seven."

"*This woman?*" asked the deputy. "And what is *this*

woman's name? Huh?" The girls looked at each other. He would never believe them. "That's what I thought," Deputy Dewayne said. He put his hands on his hips.

"I have half a mind to take you in," he said.

"But sir, we weren't doing anything," said Elizabeth. "I promise!"

"Well, get out of here then. If I find you out here again, I won't be so forgiving." He shined his flashlight in their faces, and Alexis turned around to get out of the glare. That's when she saw it. A sentence, scribbled in pencil on the white paint of the front door.

Watch beneath the moon when the bridge calls out.

●—●—●

Deputy Dewayne gave the girls a ride back to their hotels. Alexis didn't dare bring up the writing in the police car. The deputy hadn't noticed it, and she wanted to keep it that way. She didn't want him blaming them for graffiti, too. When the officer dropped off Elizabeth, Alexis waved good-bye. She would have to call Elizabeth later.

There was a note from her grandmother when she got to her room. Some old friends from Europe had come to the conference, and Grandma Windsor was going to be out with them until late. Alexis watched some old detective shows on TV Land for a while.

But her mind kept going back to the things that had happened that day. Since she had so much to think about, she got in her pajamas and climbed into her bed.

Watch beneath the moon when the bridge calls out.

What on earth did that mean? *Watch beneath the moon* was easy enough. Alexis suspected it meant to watch when the moon was shining, which would mean at night. But what about the last part? What did the woman mean, *When the bridge calls out?* Stone and cement didn't talk, as far as Alexis knew. Bridges definitely didn't *call out.*

Whatever. The lady was obviously a little crazy. And who knew? Maybe the message wasn't for the girls anyway.

Alexis looked at her clock. Too late to call Elizabeth. She would run the clue by Elizabeth tomorrow and see what she thought. She wondered if Elizabeth had gotten any e-mails from the Camp Club Girls.

Alexis rolled over onto her side. She had left the curtains and the window open to let in the fresh, cool evening air. The desert smelled wonderful at night— like cooling sage. She drifted in and out of sleep as she watched the moonbeams dance on the wall. And then she heard it: the distinct ringing of metal hitting stone, followed by a splash.

Alexis sat up, looked toward the window, and heard it again. *Ring, thump, splash.*

Was the bridge calling out?

Moonlight Sonata

Alexis pushed the covers away and scooted to the edge of her bed.

Ring, thump, splash!

What could that sound be? It was strange and muffled, as if it were coming from under a pillow. . .or water. Could this be what the writing on the old woman's door was talking about? Did she know something was happening to the bridge during the night? Alexis inched her feet down into the soft hotel carpet and tiptoed toward the window. Her grandma hadn't come back to the room yet. This and the darkness made Alexis feel very alone.

When she reached the window, the breeze stiffened and blew her unruly, bed-head hair out of her face. It was dark outside. The moon was hiding behind a large cloud. The noise had also stopped. Maybe it hadn't been the bridge. Maybe some tourists had been out late playing around the water.

Ring, thump, splash!

Alexis leaned out the window to get a better look. The strange noise was definitely coming from the bridge. The streets were empty. All the tourists and engineers were at home in their beds. She couldn't see anyone. So who—or what—was making the noise?

Alexis heard another splash, so she focused on the water. She couldn't see anything along either shore. No one was skipping rocks or taking strolls along the water's edge. Eventually she looked at the bridge again. If it was dark outside, the areas beneath the bridge were pitch-black. There was no way to see anything without some light. Alexis jumped from the window and grabbed her backpack. She rummaged through it and found what she was looking for: a flashlight.

Alexis carried the flashlight to the window and turned it on. She aimed it across the water toward the bridge. It didn't help much. The beam of light was small, and it didn't penetrate very far into the darkness under the bridge.

Splash.

Alexis turned the light toward the sound. In the second arch, near the crack, the water rippled. Had someone thrown something into the water? She looked to the top of the bridge, but still she saw no one. So what had dropped into the water? Alexis moved the light back toward the water, but it went dark.

Alexis hit the flashlight with the palm of her hand. The batteries were dead.

"Oh come on!" she whispered furiously. "You have to be kidding me!" The light flashed back on but only long enough to blind her before it went dark again.

"Kate would tell me I should have a solar-powered or hand-crank flashlight for emergencies," she muttered, almost hearing the voice of the most techno-savvy of the Camp Club Girls in her mind. "But a lot of good that does me now!"

She dropped the light and leaned out the window again, trying as hard as she could to see without it. She couldn't.

Alexis sighed and was about to go back to bed when the wind blew again. The clouds drifted out of the way, and the brilliant rays of the moon lit up Lake Havasu like it was day. Alexis couldn't believe what she saw under the bridge. Bobbing up and down on the water was a small, wooden rowboat.

That shouldn't have been surprising, since it was a lake. People rowed small boats around Lake Havasu all the time. Even at night. What confused Alexis was the fact that the small boat was empty. Had it come untied from the dock and drifted to the bridge on its own? And she still had no way to explain the noises.

Then. . .

Splash. A head emerged from the water.

Thump. Something heavy fell into the boat.

Ring. Something else fell in on top of it.

Alexis gasped. A long, dark shadow pulled itself out of the water and slid into the boat. Then it began to paddle in the opposite direction and out of sight. Alexis left the window and grabbed her notebook and a small camera she had brought for the trip. She left the room and sprinted down the hallway to the elevator.

When it opened on the first floor, Alexis ran toward the front doors. The coolness of the marble under her feet made her realize she had forgotten to put on her shoes. *Oh well*, she thought. *I've had dirty feet before.*

But when she saw the automatic doors swing open, she stopped in her tracks. Deputy Dewayne was sitting just outside in his patrol car, as if he was just waiting for her to do something like this. Alexis didn't want to cross his path for the second time in one night, so she turned around and trudged back to the elevator.

On the ride up to her floor, her mind raced. How did all of this fit together? Was it a coincidence that someone was diving in the dark beneath the bridge right where it happened to be cracked? Or could something more sinister be going on?

Alexis was sure the old woman had been trying to tell her something. Maybe she knew it wasn't really a curse. The curse could be a story made up to scare the tourists, like Dr. Edwards had said. In that case Lake Havasu City was in real trouble. Someone was trying to bring down the London Bridge. But *why?*

●—●—●

The next morning Alexis told Elizabeth everything she had seen. First about the scribbled note on the door. Then about the incident with the bridge.

"Do you really think that note was meant for us?" asked Elizabeth as they walked toward the bench near the bridge.

"I guess there's no way to know for sure," said Alexis. "We can ask the old lady the next time we see her. I really think she meant us to get it, though. I mean, she knew we were coming to see her, right?"

"Yeah," said Elizabeth, folding one long leg beneath her as she sat down. "But why on the door? Why didn't she leave another envelope or note like yesterday?"

"Well, she is a little dramatic," said Alexis. "She dresses like a medieval peasant, for goodness' sake! She's secretive, too. Maybe she was worried that an envelope taped to the door would be too obvious and that someone else would read it."

"Maybe," said Elizabeth. "We won't know until we talk to her again. So you really saw someone under the bridge last night?"

"Yep. And I just know they were banging on the bridge with some tools. Maybe a hammer or something."

"Did you see the tools?" asked Elizabeth.

"No, but I heard the banging. I saw the person drop them back into the boat when he came up, too."

"When he came up?"

"Yeah," said Alexis. "From under the water." Elizabeth looked back at the channel where dozens of engineers were busy at work again. A shifty smile spread across her face.

"You know what that means, don't you?" she said.

"What?" asked Alexis.

"It means that there really *is* a reason for us to check out the bridge! You know, like I said yesterday. We'll get some cheap goggles, and—"

"No way!" Alexis jumped off the bench. "You're

crazy! The public isn't supposed to be anywhere near the bridge! And if you haven't noticed, Elizabeth: *We're the public.* Besides, it's just plain stupid to go swimming around under a bridge that's about to collapse!"

"It's not about to collapse," said Elizabeth. "It just has a tiny crack."

"You sound like Dr. Edwards," said Alexis. "Don't you remember what the bridge commissioner said about tiny cracks? They start avalanches, Elizabeth!"

"Okay, okay! Don't freak out. You're right." Elizabeth took a deep breath and looked around. "It really isn't a good idea. So what do we do today?"

Alexis caught sight of a purple flyer taped on a lamppost.

"We haven't thought anymore about the bed race," she said. "Are you still interested?"

"Of course!" said Elizabeth. "We need a little something to distract us."

"We'd better get working on it then. The first thing we'll need is a bed."

"Good job, Einstein!" Elizabeth elbowed Alexis playfully, and the pair of girls walked toward the shopping area of downtown Lake Havasu City.

They passed a mattress shop, and Elizabeth stopped.

"This place sells beds," she said. Alexis pointed to the price tag of the small bed that was sitting in the window.

"Six hundred dollars," she said. "I think we'll need a used one."

They kept walking and turned into an older part of town. The street was narrow, more like an alley than a road. It was lined with antique shops on both sides, with a couple of coffee and pastry shops snuggled in between.

The first store they walked into was called Betsy's Boutique. It was crowded with crystal vases and candleholders and lace doilies. The girls had taken two steps into the shop when a thin woman with a birdlike nose and her hair pulled back into a tight bun stepped out from behind an ancient polished dresser.

"Where are your parents?" she asked.

"Um, back at the hotel," answered Elizabeth. The woman pointed toward a sign in the window that read NO UNATTENDED CHILDREN ALLOWED. Then she coughed and nudged them toward the door.

Back outside on the sidewalk the girls laughed.

"Well, I guess we'd better find a shop that doesn't have a problem with *unattended children*," laughed Alexis. "What about that one?" She pointed across the narrow street to a whimsical sign that said BILL'S TARNISHED TREASURES. Its windows were crowded with all kinds of things, from worn-out lamps to old bicycle seats.

"Looks good to me," said Elizabeth. They looked both ways and crossed over to the opposite sidewalk. A large jingly bell on the door announced their arrival, but nobody greeted them. In fact the store looked empty.

"Maybe they're in the back?" said Elizabeth.

"Let's look around," said Alexis. The girls didn't see a bed anywhere, but they saw plenty of other amazing things in the piles of junk. Alexis was sifting through a huge crystal bowl full of ancient brass buttons when a voice from behind her made her jump.

"That one is from a World War II naval jacket."

Alexis spun around and faced a large man in glasses. His voice was low and gentle, and his smile was warm and genuine.

"Oh," said Alexis, looking at the button she was holding. It had an anchor etched into it. "That's really neat," she said. "That makes it about. . .sixty years old."

"Just a little older, actually," said the man. "But good job! My name's Bill. This is my shop." Bill stuck out his hand, and Alexis grasped it. This was awkward, since he had a crutch under his arm.

"Nice to meet you, Bill. I'm Alexis, and this is my friend Elizabeth." Elizabeth emerged from a pile of tattered books and waved.

"It's good to meet the two of you," said Bill. "What brings you in here today? Anything in particular?"

"Well," said Alexis, "actually we're looking for a bed. We want to enter the race this weekend, but we're from out of town, and we don't, um. . .have a bed." Alexis looked around the shop. "And it doesn't look like you have one either."

Bill's face lit up, his smile stretching so wide that his glasses bounced on his large cheeks. "We're both in luck!" he said. "Follow me." He turned and hobbled past the cash register, and Alexis saw that he was wearing a full cast on one of his legs. She wondered how such a large man managed to move on crutches through such a crowded store without breaking everything in sight. Bill led them to a curtain at the back of the shop and started through it. Alexis and Elizabeth hesitated, and Bill turned around.

"Don't worry," he said. "Mary!"

"Yes, Bill?" A lovely voice floated into the room from beyond the curtain, and a pretty face followed it.

"Mary," said Bill, "this is Alexis and Elizabeth. Girls,

this is Mary, my wife. They're interested in the race, so I'm going to show them the castle!" Bill sounded like a little kid at Christmastime. Mary nodded and pointed through the curtain. The mention of a castle made the girls even more curious. They followed Bill behind the curtain, leaving it open so they could still see the door. Some of her friends called Alexis paranoid, but she got uncomfortable when she couldn't see an exit.

"Whoa," said Elizabeth.

Alexis turned around to see a huge contraption filling the tiny back room. It really was a castle! Bill had built a tower at the head of the bed, where the pillow usually went, and a low wall surrounded the rest of the mattress. At the foot, a real wooden drawbridge was closed, and a blue bed skirt fell to the floor like a rippling moat.

"This is amazing!" cried Alexis.

"Do you think so?" asked Bill. "It's taken me almost a year to build. Go ahead. Climb up and take a look!" He gestured to the back of the tower where a trapdoor revealed an entry onto the bed itself and a couple of stairs leading to the top of the tower. Alexis climbed right up.

"It feels so stable," said Alexis. "But the tower is so tall. Why doesn't it tip over?"

"Well, that's why I used real wood for the drawbridge. The tower makes the back of the bed really heavy. I needed something just as heavy to even out the weight in the front. Otherwise it would topple over the first time it went around a corner. That's also why I put *these* on it." Bill raised a corner of the bed skirt, revealing knobby tires.

"Those things look big enough to go on a tractor!" said Elizabeth.

"Close," said Bill. "They came from a riding lawn mower. The old wobbly bed wheels weren't going to work for something this huge. I also put brakes in it—something most beds in the race won't have. Once this baby gets going, it would be impossible to stop otherwise."

"I see the pedals," said Alexis. "And there's even a steering wheel!"

"Wow," said Elizabeth. "You sure put a lot into this bed. It's amazing, but I don't think we could afford to buy it from you."

Alexis sighed. She knew Elizabeth was right. There was no way they could afford a bed this cool for the race.

"It's not for sale," said Bill. "I'm giving it to you. Just for the race, I mean."

The girls were stunned.

"But why?" asked Alexis. Bill pointed to his broken leg.

"Racing is against the doctor's orders. But I'd hate to see this thing sit back here unused. And I always like to have a bed in the race representing the shop. Instead of my charging you rent, how about if you just finish the work on it and represent us? It still needs to be painted. I've got the paint. It probably wouldn't take you two very long. What do you say?"

Alexis was speechless. They hadn't even been looking for an hour, and they had found the most amazing racing bed *ever*. And they weren't going to have to pay a dime.

"Wow, Mr. Bill. I don't know what to say," said Alexis.

"Just say you'll race her hard. I'd love to be part of a winning team, even if it's just to cheer you across the finish line."

Alexis laughed and shook Bill's hand. "It's a deal!" she said. "Where are the paintbrushes?"

Alexis called her grandmother, and Elizabeth called her parents to tell them what was going on and where they were. Then they painted until late afternoon. Mary brought them turkey sandwiches for lunch and filled plastic cups with iced lemonade every twenty minutes or so.

By the time the girls began to rinse their brushes and close the cans of paint, the bed had been transformed. The walls of the castle were gray stone. White and gray paint had been sponged over it in spots to make it look real. The drawbridge was dark brown. Bill had come in with a hammer and beaten it up a little. The effect made it look weatherworn and very old. He also brought two lengths of chain and attached them to either side of the wooden bridge and then to the castle walls. They hung limp, like real chains that would allow the bridge to fall open.

A few finishing touches still needed to be done, so the girls would have to come back later in the week.

"In the meantime," said Mary as the girls prepared to leave, "Madame Brussau's is a wonderful costume shop. Your costumes should match your bed, Your Highnesses." She curtsied as if the girls were royalty.

"We will visit the shop, Madame Mary," answered Alexis. She and Elizabeth curtsied in return. "Thank you for all of your help."

All the way back to the hotel, the girls talked about their bed. Hardly any other bed would have brakes or a steering wheel, so they really felt they had a good chance of winning. That was if they could get the hang of driving the bed when they had never done it before.

Elizabeth's parents told her she could stay the night with Alexis at the London Bridge Resort. They were going to watch the bridge. Alexis hoped the person in the boat would show up again. Maybe this time they could sneak down to the water and take some pictures.

When they entered the shining lobby of the hotel, an unusual crowd surrounded the front desk. Dr. Edwards was standing across the counter from Jane. He seemed to be introducing her to two strange men in canvas work suits. They looked like painters.

Alexis motioned to Elizabeth, and the two of them slowed down. Alexis wanted to hear what they were saying as they walked past. Dr. Edwards spoke first.

"These men are Jerold and Jim," he said to Jane. "They have been hired to create a float that will represent the conference and hotel in Saturday's parade. Please allow them unlimited access to the hotel's premises, even though they are not guests. I believe your manager has left you a note to that effect."

Jane dug around on the desk in front of her. She picked up a piece of paper and studied it.

"Yep," she said. "You're good to go! This says he's set up a workroom for you near the ballroom," she said to the workmen.

"Thank you very much," said the larger of the two.

The hairs on the back of Alexis's neck stood on end. That voice. It was so familiar. Alexis waited for the man to say something else so she could place his voice, but he didn't. He only nodded and then turned and followed Dr. Edwards around the corner toward the ballroom.

Oh well. It probably just reminded her of someone back home. The two girls went upstairs, ate room service with Grandma Windsor, and went into Alexis's room to get ready for bed.

As Elizabeth opened her backpack and reached inside, Alexis saw a flash of white.

"Is that what I think it is?" she asked.

"Yep. Dad's MacBook," Elizabeth said, pulling the computer out of the canvas bag. "He said I could bring it with me tonight."

The girls put on their pajamas and then sat side by side at the computer desk in the room. Elizabeth turned on the screen, and a glowing apple appeared while the machine booted up.

When she entered the Camp Club Girls chat room, she and Alexis saw that the other girls were already there.

Bailey: *Hi Betty Boo and Lexy.*
Elizabeth: *You know I hate that name. And Lexy?*

85

That's a new one. =0

McKenzie: *We were just talking about you. Kate was telling us the stuff you texted her all day.*

Elizabeth: *Did Kate send you the photos of the bed, too?*

Sydney: *Yeah, that thing's amazing. I wish I was there to push it for you!*

McKenzie: *I don't see why they just don't race horses. Beds don't make sense. If you guys go back there next year, maybe I could come down with my horse. There's a jousting club not too far from here. Maybe I could learn to joust.*

Elizabeth: *That would be cool. Did you guys find anything out?*

Kate: *I looked up Princess Amelia. I found out that she was in love with a stable hand.*

Bailey: *Maybe he's the one who taught her to ride horses.*

Kate: *Maybe. Tradition is that she wrote him letters. After she died, the stories say he couldn't find her last letter. He spent the rest of his life looking for it.*

McKenzie: *What happened to him?*

Kate: *Well, actually he died not too long after*

Amelia. Of some sort of plague.

Sydney: *That happened a lot in those times. People died suddenly. He might even have died in the saddle!*

Bailey: *What are you going to do next?*

Elizabeth: *As I texted you earlier today, Alexis saw weird stuff at the bridge last night. We're going to try to keep an eye on the bridge tonight.*

Kate: *Do you have your automatic recording camera with you that you used at Miss Maria's nature park? You know—when you were trying to catch the dinosaurs in action? If so, you can set it up to try to catch any action.*

Elizabeth: *No, we don't have one of those.*

Kate: *Do you want me to overnight a spycam to you?*

Elizabeth: *I think we'll be okay.*

●—●—●

When the girls got off the computer, they weren't tired at all. On the contrary, they were quite excited. They sat at the window for hours waiting for the mysterious person in the rowboat.

He didn't come.

It was one o'clock in the morning, and both girls were asleep on the windowsill. Suddenly Alexis jumped.

"What?" said Elizabeth, immediately awake. "Did you see something?"

"No," said Alexis. "That man in the lobby! I just remembered where I've heard his voice before!"

"Oh. Where?" asked Elizabeth. She relaxed back into her chair.

"Elizabeth, I heard it in the alley! Remember? The two voices were talking about—"

"No way!" Elizabeth sat straight up again.

"Yes way! I have no idea how they are going to do it, but those two men are going to steal the golden coach!"

CHAPTER 7

Priceless or Useless

The girls had breakfast in the hotel restaurant with Alexis's grandma. Alexis still didn't feel the girls had enough information to tell her grandmother what was happening. Still, she was nervous about the speculations she and Elizabeth had. The fact that the con men had gotten jobs at the hotel would make it easier for them to steal the carriage. She had *no* idea how they could do it, but it still worried her.

Alexis knew her grandma would know what to do, but she still didn't feel confident enough to tell her everything. She wondered what she would say about the *idea* of the carriage being stolen.

"Grandma," said Alexis, as the waitress filled her glass of orange juice. "Why is there so little security around the carriage? What would happen if someone tried to steal it?"

Grandma Windsor chuckled.

"Darling, that carriage is huge! No one would be

able to get it out of the hotel unnoticed. But even if they could, what would they do with it?"

"Well, it's valuable, isn't it?" asked Elizabeth.

"In its own way, yes," said Grandma Windsor. "But I don't see why anyone would want it. It's the only replica of its kind, so you couldn't sell it to anyone. It would be too easy for the police to track it down again."

"Well, what about a collector or something? Someone like you, who really likes history and stuff?" asked Alexis. She was remembering the many old trinkets her grandmother brought back from her travels. Her house was full of them. Again Grandma Windsor laughed.

"A *real* collector or historian wouldn't want a replica. Deep down, it's only a fake. Would a literature professor be content with a new version of Shakespeare, if there was a possibility they could hold the original? No. Anyone can walk into a bookstore and get a copy of *Romeo and Juliet* for less than five dollars. But the original? Priceless."

"So replicas are worthless?" asked Alexis.

"Now, I didn't say that," said Grandma Windsor. "Take Michelangelo's statue of David, for instance. If you walk up to the statue in the plaza, you will enjoy its beauty. You may take pictures and go on your merry way, but if that's as far as you went, then you missed the truth. You have only seen a replica—a smaller shadow of the true art of Michelangelo. The real statue is inside, hidden away from the damaging elements. But the replica is not worthless, Alexis. It is still beautiful; it's just not *as* beautiful. It does not have the same history."

The waitress was back, refilling Grandma Windsor's glass of tea this time.

"So, besides the fact that it is almost impossible to get the coach out of this building unnoticed, I simply don't see why someone would want to steal it in the first place. That is why there isn't much security around it. The hotel has never felt that it was threatened."

But it is *threatened!* Alexis wanted to scream. But after all Grandma Windsor had just said, she thought it would sound silly to voice her thoughts.

After they finished eating, the girls left Grandma Windsor and walked toward Bill and Mary's shop. The bridge was still crawling with engineers, and they would have to wait until night before looking for the rowboat again. So no matter how tempting the mystery surrounding the bridge was, Alexis was going to focus on the carriage for a while.

Alexis knew Jerold and Jim were the same people she had overheard in the alley earlier in the week. But she was starting to have doubts about other things. Would it really be possible for Jerold and Jim, those silly-looking "float builders," to steal the golden coach? There was *no way* they could remove it without someone noticing. As soon as it was missing, someone would sound the alarm. They wouldn't make it very far.

And *why* were they planning to steal it in the first place? They had said it was worth millions, but Grandma Windsor claimed the carriage wasn't worth much at all. Sure, it was probably expensive to make, but you could always build another one. It wasn't like the original coach back in London, which was covered with real gold.

"There's only one way to know for sure if they are going to steal the carriage," said Alexis as they turned down the narrow street to Bill's. "We have to *investigate* these two guys."

"You mean spy on them?" asked Elizabeth, smiling.

"Well, yes," laughed Alexis. "*Investigating* just sounds a lot better! We'll work on the bed for a bit and then go back to the hotel. They're making the float near the ballroom. It shouldn't be too hard to find them."

In the back room of the antique shop, the girls admired their castle. It only needed a couple of touch-ups. Alexis was attaching fake fish to the bed skirt-moat when the bell on the front door jingled. She heard a girl's voice say, "Hello, Uncle Bill."

The voice didn't sound friendly.

Alexis and Elizabeth poked their heads through the curtain and saw a slim brunette standing with her hands on her hips.

"Hello, Emily," said Bill. "Shouldn't you be in school?"

"I heard you have someone driving your bed," the girl said, ignoring his question. Her face was scrunched up, like she smelled something gross.

"Yep, sure do," said Bill. He sounded friendly, but his stiff shoulders told Alexis he had put his guard up. "What brings you down here? Need something for a costume?"

"Eew, gross! Like I would use any of this junk for my costume!" Emily picked up a silver teaspoon with her forefinger and thumb, like it was covered in grime.

"I don't understand what makes you love other people's old stuff so much. Like this spoon." She held it up to the light and then looked around the table where it had been sitting. "It's all dingy, and there's only *one*.

93

What on earth would anyone do with only one spoon?"

"Actually, if you look at the handle—"

But Emily didn't. She rolled her eyes and tossed the spoon toward Bill. He fumbled, and it fell to the ground. Alexis stepped through the curtain to pick it up and hand it to him.

"Who are *you*?" asked Bill's demanding niece.

"This is Alexis," said Bill. "She's the one racing my bed this Saturday."

Alexis smiled and waved. Emily's eyes narrowed to tiny slits.

"Well, she'd better be careful," she said, stepping closer. "The driver who tried to beat me last year ended up in the hospital with a broken arm. And I *don't lose.*"

Emily turned and stormed out of the shop. Alexis was sure she would have slammed the door if it hadn't been for the automatic spring that caught it and made it close gently.

"What was that all about?" asked Elizabeth.

"Oh, don't mind Emily," said Bill. "She's just mad because I wouldn't let her use my bed in the race. She thought I would for sure, since she's family. My brother's kid. Ever heard the term 'spoiled rotten'? Well, that's Emily for sure."

"Why wouldn't you let her race it?" asked Alexis.

"You heard her, didn't you?" said Bill. "She put a guy in the hospital last year—slammed into his bed on the last turn and sent him flying into the crowd. You're not supposed to touch anyone else's bed. Emily told the judges it was an accident, and they believed her and gave her the prize."

"But you didn't believe it was an accident?" asked Alexis.

"Do you, Alexis? I can't have anyone representing my shop doing risky things that might bring bad publicity."

Bill was right. Alexis had just met Emily, and she was pretty sure Emily would have broken someone's arm to get what she wanted.

"Well, she can have the prize for all I care," said Alexis. "I just want to race!"

"That's right," said Elizabeth. "It's like Psalm 37:1 says, 'Do not fret because of evil men or be envious of those who do wrong.' No matter what happens, we'll have a blast."

"*And* you'll have the best bed out there!" said Bill. "That thing should be in the parade! It'll be better than any other float!"

Bill still held the small spoon that Emily had tossed

at him. He placed it on the table, but Alexis picked it up.

"What were you about to say about the spoon, Bill—before Emily interrupted you?" asked Alexis. Bill smiled. It reminded Alexis of her grandmother's smile when she asked her about history.

"Look at the handle," he said. Alexis held the spoon up in the light, and Elizabeth came close to look as well. A small pink stone shaped like an oval was mounted on the end of the handle. Upon the oval stone a face had been carved. It was the silhouette of a young beautiful woman.

"Who is it?" asked Elizabeth.

"Princess Amelia, the youngest daughter of—"

"King George the Third!" gasped Alexis.

"You've heard her story then?" asked Bill.

"Pieces of it," answered Alexis. "My grandmother told me some of the stories surrounding her. Something about Princess Amelia and a young man she was forbidden to marry."

"That's what she is most known for," said Bill. "They say the law would have allowed her to marry him after she turned twenty-six, but that was pretty old to be married back then. Her letters may have told him that she would wait. If she hid a letter to give him, no one knows if he ever found it. This spoon is a rare piece.

Since Princess Amelia was never a queen, it is quite strange for silverware to have her picture on it. Maybe she really was her father's favorite."

"Wow!" said Alexis. "That means this spoon is more than two hundred years old!"

"Why do you keep that out on a table?" asked Elizabeth. "Shouldn't it be locked away somewhere?"

Bill laughed.

"Probably. A lot of the stuff in my store is more valuable than people think. Like Emily, many think it's just junk—like an indoor yard sale."

"Well, I think it's brilliant," said Alexis. She looked at the spoon again. Was it just her imagination, or did the picture on the spoon look like the girl from her dream? Her imagination was running wild again.

"Hey, look!" cried Elizabeth. Alexis followed her pointed finger toward the large window. Outside, three familiar figures were walking through the alley.

"It's Dr. Edwards—and those two workmen from the hotel!" Alexis looked at Elizabeth and lowered her voice so Bill couldn't hear. "If we follow them, we might find out more about their plan for the carriage."

"They probably won't talk about it with Dr. Edwards around," said Elizabeth. "Maybe he'll leave."

Alexis nodded. "See ya later," she said to Bill. "It's

getting to be lunchtime."

"I'm getting hungry myself," said the shop owner. "See you girls later."

Alexis and Elizabeth waved good-bye and left the shop. They were just in time to see the end of Dr. Edwards's walking stick disappear around a corner. They followed, and after a couple of turns their prey entered a small deli.

"Well, it *is* lunchtime," said Alexis. "Feel like a sandwich?" Elizabeth smiled. The girls allowed a couple more people to enter before they did. They didn't want to be directly behind Dr. Edwards in line in case he recognized them.

After ordering turkey sandwiches and grabbing a couple bags of chips, Alexis led Elizabeth to a booth that hid them from the three men but was still close enough so they could hear everything that was being said.

"I thought you said this job was going to be easy," said the taller of the two men.

"I thought the job was going to be easy, Jerold," said Dr. Edwards. "But circumstances have changed."

"Well, I hope we're getting paid more," said Jerold.

"Yes, yes," said Dr. Edwards testily. "Don't worry about the money! It will come!"

"I don't know what you want with that thing anyway," said another voice. It must have been Jim. "It's a fake. How can it be worth much money?"

Dr. Edwards sighed. Alexis was sure that if she could see him, his eyes would be bulging in exasperation.

"It's not the carriage itself that is priceless," he said, dropping his voice to a whisper. Alexis had to stop chewing her chips so that she could still hear him. "It's something hidden within it."

Alexis stared across the table at Elizabeth. She, too, had stopped chewing. They sat still, straining to hear every word.

"I have reason to believe that an original document, hundreds of years old, has been hidden somewhere within the carriage. The *document*, my dear fellows, is what's priceless. The carriage just happens to be the hiding place."

The thieves seemed to be happy with the doctor's explanation, because all Alexis and Elizabeth heard after that was the chomping and slurping of the two men eating.

The girls finished their food and slipped out the front.

"So *that's* why Dr. Edwards wants the carriage! He thinks something is hidden inside of it!" said Elizabeth.

"Yeah," said Alexis. "A priceless document. What if it was Princess Amelia's letter?"

"Why would Princess Amelia's letter be hidden in a *replica*?" asked Elizabeth. "The real carriage, maybe, but there's no reason for it to be in Arizona. Your imagination's running away with you again, Alex."

"You're right," said Alexis. "But wouldn't it be cool? No matter what the document is, it's obviously worth a lot of money. *And* it has a rightful owner. I bet if Dr. Edwards were the rightful owner, he wouldn't have to steal it."

"I know," said Elizabeth. "We have to keep him from stealing it. But how are we supposed to do that when we don't know where it is?"

"Easy," said Alexis, smiling wide. "We just have to find it before he does."

Encounter in the Costume Shop

"How on earth are we supposed to do that?" asked Elizabeth. "You saw how that deputy guy reacted when we were just looking at the carriage. What do you think will happen if we actually try to *touch* the thing? Or search it for an ancient letter?"

"We'll just have to be careful," said Alexis. "It might be difficult, but we don't have a choice. If the document exists, it belongs in a museum—not in Dr. Edwards's personal collection."

They walked toward the hotel, thinking about how best to search for the hidden paper. Alexis was so deep in thought that she ran right into a sidewalk display in front of the costume store. She and Elizabeth struggled to dust off the white, curly wigs and hang them back up before anyone noticed.

"Let's go in here," said Alexis. "We need costumes for the bed race and parade, don't we?"

"Definitely!" squealed Elizabeth. They walked in

and were immediately hidden in a maze of silk dresses, old-fashioned shoes, and jesters' hats.

"It looks like it's almost all medieval," said Elizabeth.

"Good," said Alexis. "We have to match our bed. It's a castle. What do you think we should be?"

"We could be knights," said Elizabeth, walking over to a suit of armor. "This looks so real!"

"It also looks like it weighs a hundred pounds!" laughed Alexis. They continued through the store, yelling back and forth whenever they found something interesting. Before long they were trying on everything they could reach, making each other collapse in fits of giggles. Alexis grabbed a garish jester's hat with six floppy tentacles and jingle bells everywhere. She smashed it onto her head and spun around.

"Classy, huh?" she asked Elizabeth. But the person behind her wasn't Elizabeth.

It was David Turner, the Arizona state swim champion.

"Very classy," he said, raising his eyebrows and giving her an amused smile. Alexis blushed. It was the first time she'd ever seen David smile. He was twice as cute when he did. She wondered why he never smiled at swim meets or in front of his school.

Alexis yanked the hat off her head but was instantly

aware of how messed up her hair must be.

"Um, sorry," she said. "I thought my friend was standing there."

She looked around frantically. Where was Elizabeth anyway?

"Don't apologize," said David. "I wouldn't expect any less of someone visiting a costume shop." He was still smiling, as if whatever bothered him at other times was now forgotten.

"I'm Alexis," she said, holding out her hand. David had to rearrange the things he was holding to shake her hand. He dropped a large sword, and they banged heads as they both reached to pick it up.

"Ow!" said Alexis.

"Sorry!" he said, rubbing his head and wiping his long hair out of his eyes at the same time. "You look familiar. Have I met you before?"

"No," said Alexis. "My friend and I went to the swim meet the other day."

"No, that's not it," he said. "Dude! You're the girl from the pep rally!"

Alexis turned crimson. "That was an accident," she said hastily. "My friend and I don't even go to school here!"

"Oh," said the boy. "You don't?" Was Alexis

imagining things, or did he look disappointed?

"It's a long story," she said. "We just ended up in the building by accident."

"Well, you're a legend anyway. The whole school's talking about you."

"Great," said Alexis. They both laughed. Then there was an embarrassing silence. Alexis twisted the jester's hat in her hands, and David placed the sword back in a display.

"Not going to get it?" Alexis asked.

"Nope," he said. "I think I'm going to go with the dragon." He held up the head of a costume that was piled under his right arm.

Just then a horrible screech came from outside, followed by a loud crash. Alexis turned and ran to the sidewalk with David just behind her. Elizabeth wasn't far behind. Right in front of the store, two cars were stopped. Apparently one of the drivers hadn't been paying attention and had slammed into the car ahead. Both bumpers were crushed, and the back car was smoking a bit.

The drivers stumbled out of their vehicles and began yelling at each other. No one was hurt, but neither person wanted to take the blame. Within minutes two police cars showed up and a sheriff approached the arguing drivers.

Someone tapped Alexis on the shoulder.

"Trespassing wasn't enough?" a voice said. "Now you have to shoplift, too?"

Alexis spun around to see Deputy Dewayne inches from her face.

"What? Shoplifting?" she stammered. The deputy pointed to her arms. Alexis was still carrying the jester's hat. She looked side to side. David still had his dragon costume, and Elizabeth was holding a pink dress and had a matching crown on her head. None of the items had been paid for.

"Oh this," said Alexis. "We were just looking inside the store when the crash happened. We ran outside to see what happened and forgot we were holding it all."

Deputy Dewayne didn't move.

"Really, Deputy," said David. "She's telling the truth. We were just about to pay."

The officer's eyes narrowed, and then he spun around as the sheriff called his name. Alexis, Elizabeth, and David took that opportunity to slide back into the store and head for the cash register.

Elizabeth had found a great princess costume. Alexis found a crazy outfit that matched her jester's hat. She had wanted to be a princess, too, but she loved the hat too much to part with it. They paid and turned to go.

"Uh, see you later?" said David from behind them. His dragon costume was on the counter.

"Yeah, later," said Alexis. She turned and led Elizabeth out the door.

"Um, Alexis?" said Elizabeth.

"Yeah?"

"I think that was a question."

"What do you mean?" asked Alexis.

"What David said just now—I think it was a question. Like, *Can I see you later?* Not, *See ya later.* Get the difference?"

Alexis stopped in her tracks, blushing from the neck all the way up to her ponytail. Her eyes were dinner plates.

"No way!" she said.

"I could be wrong," said Elizabeth. "But it seemed like he liked you."

"What do I do?" said Alexis, frantic. "I don't want him to think I was rude!"

"Go talk to him. He's coming out of the store right now."

Alexis turned around. "David!" she called. He spun around, yanking a pair of earbuds out of his ears so he could hear her.

"Yeah?"

"Um, do you want to hang out with us? I mean, we're not doing anything really, just walking around."

"I've got swim practice now. Maybe later?"

"Tomorrow, maybe," said Alexis. "If not, we'll be in the bed race. Look for the amazing castle."

"Okay," said David, smiling shyly. "See ya."

This time she was sure it was "see ya later." Alexis waved and turned back to Elizabeth, smiling like she had just won a million dollars.

"Chill out!" said Elizabeth. "Take a deep breath. He's a boy, not Superman!" Alexis laughed.

"So what now?" she asked.

"We could try to find out more about the piece of paper Dr. Edwards is looking for," said Elizabeth.

"That's a good idea," said Alexis. "We should check out the area at the hotel where those guys are building the float. We might overhear something else—or at least get an idea of where to look."

Back at the hotel the girls asked Jane for directions to the ballroom. As they approached it, they heard the *tick, tick, tick* of someone shaking a can of spray paint. It was coming from a door across the hall. Fumes and voices drifted out to where the girls were standing.

The door was open a couple of feet, so the girls

walked up and peeked inside. Jerold and Jim were working on what Alexis guessed was the float. It was a perfect model of the carriage in the lobby, except that it was white. Alexis waved a hand at Elizabeth to get her to follow, and then she ducked inside and hid behind a tower of empty buckets.

No one saw them come in.

Jerold put down the spray paint he had been using and turned to call across the room.

"Oy! Jim! Hurry up with that stuff, eh? We ain't got all day!"

"I'm a comin', I'm a comin'! Hold yer horses!"

Alexis and Elizabeth held their breath. Jim's voice was just on the other side of the buckets. They heard him rustle around some more and then tromp off toward where the carriage and Jerold waited in the center of the room.

Relieved, Alexis looked through a gap between two buckets so she could see what was going on. Jim had a large roll of something in his hand. It looked like aluminum foil, except that it was gold instead of silver.

"Be careful, dimwit!" yelled Jerold. "You're making it flake! We can't have pieces of gold missing!"

"Why are we doing this, anyway?" asked Jim. "If the boss wants some old paper, why doesn't he just get it out of the carriage while everyone's asleep? We could do that easy!"

"Because it's not just lying on top of the velvet cushion, stupid. It's in a hidden compartment, and he doesn't know where it is. He needs more time to search."

"So how is a carriage float going to help?" asked Jim.

"Are you really that dim?" said Jerold, smacking Jim upside the head. But he didn't say anything else. Alexis and Elizabeth hid for almost an hour, but the conversation was over. Both men were intent on covering the carriage float with the golden foil.

Alexis was with Jim. She didn't see how this float was going to help Dr. Edwards find the document he was looking for. They needed more information. Alexis felt like she had a lot of clues, but none of them seemed to fit together.

Were the Camp Club Girls at a dead end?

David's Story

Bailey: *Lex, I really like your court jester hat.*
Are you and Bets going to be in a costume contest?
Alexis: *How do you know about my costume?*
Bailey: *K8 forwarded the photos of you trying on*
the hats.
Sydney: *Who was that hottie standing*
behind you?
Alexis: *Beth? How could she be standing behind*
me if she was taking pictures? And since
when do you call her a hottie?
Sydney: *Not her, goofy. The dude.*
Bailey: *Was he the Man of La Mancha or whatever?*
Sydney: *What's that?*
Alexis: *Oh, I saw that old movie. It was about*
Don Quixote.
Sydney: *Who's that?*
Alexis: *Some knight in search of adventure.*
Kate: *I believe that was during the Spanish*

Inquisition—in a different country and a different century than King George's time.

Sydney: *Well, he may not be the Man of La Mancha, but I definitely think he's the man of la macho!*

Alexis: *He is cute. And he was really nice in the costume store. You'd like him, Sydney—he's a champion swimmer. But he's been kind of surly the other times I've seen him.*

Bailey: *Surly? What's that?*

Alexis: *Grouchy.*

Kate: *Beth just texted me that you're blushing bright red when you're talking or writing about Daaaavvviiiddd.*

Bailey: *Wait, where's Betty Boo? And who's David?*

Alexis: *She's right here. But I have control of the keyboard, and I'm not giving it up. . . . Mwah-ha-ha. . . (That's an evil laugh, Bailey. And you better be glad she doesn't have control of anything if you're calling her Betty Boo again. She hates that.) And David's the guy in the photo.*

Bailey: *Oh, Groucho—the guy who's the swimmer.*

McKenzie: *So. . . Don't avoid the subject. Why do you blush when the guy's around? Are you and he going to the festivities dressed as Princess*

Amelia and her horse trainer?

Bailey: *Do you think Groucho has anything to do with the mystery?*

Alexis: *Oh no. I'm sure he doesn't.*

Bailey: *But you saw someone in the water a couple of nights ago. If he's a swimmer, could that have been him?*

Alexis: *That late at night? It was a school night. What would a kid not much older than us be doing out at that time of night?*

Bailey: *Well, if he's the swim-meister of the century. . .*

Alexis: *I don't think so. I think it has something to do with Dr. Edwards and with the cursing woman.*

Bailey: *She uses bad language?*

Alexis: *No, she is the one who was saying there's a curse on the bridge. I think adults are running this thing.*

Kate: *Well, I researched Dr. Edwards, and he's legit. I couldn't find anything suspicious about him. I even checked his photo from the past against one Beth snapped and sent to us the other day, and it was definitely the same guy who's listed all over the Internet with all kinds of credentials.*

Sydney: *I asked my aunt—you know, who works*

with the park services—if she knew anything
about any funny business in that area.
She says the rangers in the region have never
mentioned anything.

Alexis: *We're stuck. I keep trying to think of what*
Sherlock Holmes or Hercule Poirot or
McGyver or Jessica Fletcher would do.

Bailey: *Who are they?*

Sydney: *They're fictional detectives.*

Bailey: *Oh. Or Scooby Doo, Shaggy, Velma,*
and Daphne.

Alexis: *Yeah or even them. I'm sure I've seen*
something on one of those mystery shows that
should ring a bell and remind me of one of
their plots, but I'm stumped. Ebeth just
reminded me we have to go. Have to do a
final check on the bed. Will send more photos
later. Keep thinking. . . .

●—●—●

As Alexis and Elizabeth walked back to Bill's shop,
they kept trying to figure out what was going on. No
matter how exciting the investigation was getting, they
had to admit that they were stuck.

Then they were at the shop. As Alexis looked at the
bed, she paced back and forth biting her nails.

"I wish we could test-drive it!" Alexis said. She was more than a little nervous about driving in a race when she had never even sat behind the steering wheel of a go-cart.

"I'll push," said Elizabeth. "You can steer. My legs are longer, so I can push and ride at the same time—almost like a scooter."

Alexis almost protested, but when she stopped pacing, she realized that the back of the bed came up to her waist. There was no way she'd be able to jump on when the bed got going very fast.

She was going to have to steer.

Bill climbed up into the front of the bed and called her up, too. Since they had been here last, Bill and Mary had made a driver's seat. It was an old recliner painted gold to look like a throne.

"This is the steering wheel, obviously," said Bill, pointing. Alexis sat on the edge of the throne and grasped the wheel so hard her knuckles turned white.

"Mr. Bill," said Alexis. "I would love to be able to say that I drive on a regular basis, but I'm twelve." Bill laughed.

"Well, have you ever played one of those racing video games? The huge ones with wheels and pedals?"

"A couple of times," said Alexis.

"You'll be fine then. There's only one pedal on this one though. That's the brake." He pointed his foot below the chair, and Alexis saw the black pedal. It was as big as her foot. *Good*, she thought. *There's no way I'll miss it.*

Alexis turned the steering wheel and pressed the pedal over and over. If she could just get used to it, maybe she wouldn't be so afraid in the morning. She wished she had more strength in her legs.

Maybe I should take up swimming or something, she thought. That reminded her of David.

"Hey, Mr. Bill, do you know David Turner?"

"Yes, I've met him," Mr. Bill replied. "Good kid."

"It seems like he doesn't smile too often," said Alexis. "And I noticed at the swim meet the other day that other people had family members around to congratulate them, but he didn't. He just stood there looking grouchy."

Mary walked into the room with some glasses and a pitcher full of lemonade for the girls.

"Poor kid," she said. "David lost his parents and sister a year or so ago in a car wreck." She handed each of the girls a glass and started pouring out the cool yellow treat. "David wasn't in the car because he was at a swim meet. He lives with his uncle Jeff. Jeff is a good

115

man, but he isn't married and doesn't know what it's like to be a parent. He works a lot of hours, so David's left alone a lot. Often at night, even," she explained. "I understand money is a problem for them, too. I've noticed that David is smiling more lately. It's tough to lose your parents.

"I know David's coach, too. He told me meets are really hard for David sometimes. Especially when he wins. His parents were on the way to his meet when they had the wreck. It was hard for him to keep swimming. But he does love it and is so good at it. They've thought about training him for the Olympics even if he is a little old for starting that," she added.

"The swim-meister," Elizabeth murmured.

The front door jingled as someone entered. Seconds later, Emily's better-than-you voice drifted through the curtain.

"Hey, Uncle Bill," she called. "You ready to lose tomorrow?"

Bill sighed and walked into the shop. Alexis and Elizabeth climbed off the bed and followed.

"We're ready to race, if that's what you mean," said Alexis. She smiled, hoping to get a similar reaction out of Emily.

"'Do not answer a fool according to his folly, or you

will be like him yourself,'" Elizabeth murmured.

Alexis smiled. "Proverbs?"

"Yep, 26:4."

Emily did smile at Alexis's comment all right, but it was not a smile of kindness.

"Mmm," she said. "Where's your third, anyway?"

"Our what?" asked Elizabeth.

"Your third. You know, your other person." Alexis and Elizabeth looked at each other, confused. "Don't tell me you don't know!" squealed Emily. Alexis thought she sounded a little too pleased. Emily dug a folded purple paper out of her back pocket. As she unfolded it, Alexis recognized it as one of the bed race flyers.

"Didn't you read the small print?" asked Emily. She pointed to the very bottom of the flyer. "All teams must be made up of three or four people. No more, no less." She refolded the flyer and looked at them with a smile.

"See you in the morning!" Emily chirped, then she turned and left.

Alexis looked back and forth between Elizabeth and Bill. What were they going to do?

"Mr. Bill, can you ride with us?" asked Elizabeth. "I'm sure we could make it safe enough. We'll go slow!"

"No way, girls," he answered. "That's kind of you, but if you went slow enough to keep my leg from getting hurt, you'd have no chance at winning."

"We'd rather race slowly than not race at all!" said Alexis.

"You'll find someone else," said Bill. "There are tons of people in this town willing to jump on a bed just for the ride."

"What about Miss Mary?" asked Elizabeth.

The woman's voice floated from behind the cash register. "Someone has to keep the store open for the tourists," she said.

Alexis and Elizabeth couldn't believe their luck. They had worked so hard on finishing this bed and had been so excited to race. Now it looked like they might not even be able to. Alexis took a deep breath. There was no way she was giving up this easily.

"Come on, Elizabeth," she said. "We've got to find a partner."

"Well, you know what Matthew 7:7 says," Elizabeth pointed out. "'Seek and you will find!'"

The girls waved at Bill and Mary. "We'll see you bright and early," said Bill. "Don't worry. Not only will your bed race, but it will win if I can do anything about it!"

The girls practically ran back to the hotel. But before long they were sitting outside on the curb sulking. They had run out of options. Grandma

Windsor was riding on the hotel float with Dr. Edwards. Elizabeth's dad was riding on the bass float, since he won third place in the tournament. And Elizabeth's brother had eaten too much cotton candy and was sick. That meant her mom was staying with him at their hotel. Alexis even asked Jane, the lady at the front desk, but she had to work.

Alexis was trying to be upbeat, but she was really disappointed.

"Excuse me, ma'am!" Alexis called to a complete stranger walking past them. "Would you like to ride with us in the bed race tomorrow?" The lady gave her a funny look and shook her head. Then she walked away mumbling something in a foreign language.

Elizabeth laughed.

"Well, at least I tried!" said Alexis. She couldn't help but laugh, too. Something would come up; she just knew it would. There was no way they weren't going to race tomorrow.

After twenty minutes or so the girls decided to take a walk before dinner. They headed toward the bridge and were surprised to find that no one was there. The caution tape was still up, but the engineers were all gone.

"I wonder where they all went," said Elizabeth.

"Me, too," said Alexis. "Why aren't the engineers working? Don't they care if the town has to cancel the parade?"

They were walking past the bridge to the harbor when Alexis saw him. David Turner. He turned onto the street a few blocks ahead of them, hands shoved in his pockets and his hood pulled up over his head.

"Elizabeth, look! It's David!"

"Okay, okay! Calm down! Remember, Alex, he's just a boy."

"No, it's not *that*!" said Alexis, blushing. "The race! I bet he'd ride with us. Come on!" Alexis pulled Elizabeth by the elbow and walked even faster.

"David!" Alexis called, but he didn't turn around. "I bet he has his earbuds in." They sped up even more, trying to catch up, but wherever David was off to, it seemed like he was in a hurry.

"That's odd," said Elizabeth. "Is he pulling a wagon?"

"I think he is," said Alexis. Sure enough, David was pulling a red metal wagon behind him. "What could he possibly be doing with that?" asked Alexis.

David came to a stop near the harbor. He turned onto the wooden pier, wheeling his wagon along with him. When the girls caught up, he was on his knees digging around in a rowboat that was bobbing up and down in the water.

"Hey, David," said Alexis. "How are you—"

Alexis almost screamed. She was looking over David's shoulder into the small rowboat. When he moved an old tarp aside, she saw a chisel and a hammer along with some snorkeling gear. Next to the tools was a large pile of stones from the London Bridge.

Rocks in the Boat

"What is all of this?" squealed Alexis. The music from David's earbuds thrummed. He couldn't hear her. Alexis reached out and tapped him firmly on the shoulder. He spun around so fast that he almost lost his balance and fell in the water.

"Alexis!" he yelled, pulling the device from his ears. "I didn't see you there. You scared me."

David looked between the two girls. Elizabeth's mouth hung open in shock. Alexis's face was scrunched up in fury.

"Bailey was right! It's been you the whole time!" she yelled, pointing her finger in his face. David's mouth opened and closed like a fish out of water. It looked like he wanted to say something but couldn't quite find the words. "You've been the one tearing the London Bridge apart! You're responsible for the crack!"

"What are you talking about?" asked David. "I'm not tearing the bridge apart."

"Then where did those stones come from?" asked Elizabeth. David looked over his shoulder to the pile of stones in the rowboat. There was no doubt—they were the same gray, weathered stones that built the bridge.

"These are from the bridge, but they're just samples," said David. "One of the engineers asked me if I could gather some of the stones for testing. He was supposed to come down here and get them this afternoon."

David seemed like he was being completely honest, but Alexis didn't like the sound of his story. Why would an engineer ask a teenager to take apart a bridge? Didn't they have their own people to do that stuff? Well, the story might sound shifty, but Alexis thought David was telling the truth. He believed he was helping, not hurting the bridge. There was one way to find out for sure.

"When did this *engineer* ask you to do this?" asked Alexis. Her face softened, and she was no longer glaring at him.

"About two weeks ago. It takes about two days for me to get one stone loose."

"And didn't you notice you were causing a crack to appear in the bridge?" said Elizabeth.

"I do my work at night, because I'm so busy during

the day. And I wanted to make some extra money to help my uncle pay bills. I wanted to surprise him, so I've been working at night, while he's at work. I never saw the crack until earlier this week, when people started making such a fuss. I asked the engineer about it the last time I saw him, but he said not to worry about it." David turned to Elizabeth. "Why are you looking at me like that?" he asked.

Alexis turned around and looked at her friend. Elizabeth was still looking suspicious. Her eyes were narrow, and her arms were crossed. One of her feet at the end of a long leg was tap, tap, tapping on the wood of the dock.

"No offense, David," Elizabeth said, "but your story sounds crazy. You said you were supposed to meet this engineer today? Well, where is he?"

David looked up the street toward town.

"I'm not sure." He glanced at his watch. "He's late."

"Well," said Alexis, "the engineers who are taking care of the bridge are staying at my hotel. We could go see if he's there. Then you could give him the stones, and we can clear all this up."

"Sounds good to me," said David. "You wanna help me put these things in the wagon? I doubt we'd be able to carry them all the way."

One by one they piled the old stones into the wagon. They were as gentle as possible. The last thing they wanted to do was break one of them in half. Twenty minutes later they were pulling the wagon into the lobby of the London Bridge Resort. The tourists and workers alike turned to watch them wheel the wagon toward the front desk.

"Hi, Jane," said Alexis. "Do you know where the head engineer is right now?"

"I believe the engineers are eating a late lunch," she said, pointing toward the restaurant at the front of the lobby. "What's in the wagon?"

Alexis didn't answer. She turned and led Elizabeth and David toward a nearby table where a team of men in jeans and white polo shirts were eating.

"Um, excuse me," she said. The men stopped chewing and looked at her. One of them sat frozen with his sandwich halfway to his open mouth. "We're looking for one of your engineers."

The men looked back and forth at one another, surprised. Then the one with his sandwich halfway to his mouth answered her.

"I'm the chief engineer, name's Cliff. Which one of my men are you looking for?" Alexis looked at David, since he was the one who knew whom they were looking for.

"I don't remember his name," he said, "but I think it started with a *J*."

"I'm John," said a thin man at the end of the table with a bowl of pasta in front of him.

David looked at Alexis and shook his head. The man he was looking for was not at the table.

"This is all of us," said Cliff. "Is there something I can help you with?"

"Well," said Alexis, "some engineer told David that he would pay him to take samples from the bridge for testing. They're right here." She gestured toward the wagon, and Cliff's sandwich dropped onto his plate with a *splat*.

"These are from the bridge? The *London Bridge*?" David nodded.

"Where did you take them from?" asked Cliff, excited. He jumped up and flew to the wagon, picking up the stones one by one.

"The second pillar, under the waterline," said David. "That's where the engineer told me to take them from."

"Let's get one thing straight," said Cliff. "A true engineer would never tell a kid to remove stonework from a bridge—especially an historical bridge like this one. I think you got duped, kid."

"I don't understand," said David. "The guy was so—"

"Wait!" yelled Cliff. "Did you say you took these from the second pillar?"

"Yeah," said David.

"Right under where the crack appeared?" said another engineer with gravy all over his chin. David nodded.

Cliff jumped out of his seat.

"John, Matt—finish eating, then check this out. I believe this explains the crack. If so, then there's no real damage. These stones can be replaced, and the crack can be filled. It's only surface damage!"

Cliff called over to where Jane was standing at the front desk. "Call the mayor! Tell him the parade is on!" Everyone in the restaurant and hotel lobby erupted in applause. After a minute, David's voice broke through the commotion.

"Excuse me, sir," he said. Cliff turned back toward the three young people. Alexis and Elizabeth were glad that the parade would go on, but David looked troubled.

"I feel stupid," he said. "I should have known that pulling chunks off the bridge wasn't right, but the guy was so convincing. Why would he want these rocks anyway?"

"Don't worry, son," said Cliff. "I believe that you

didn't mean to cause any harm. You're no danger to anyone. The person who is a danger is that man who talked you into this. If you see him around, don't let him know we're on to him. You come find me, and we'll get the sheriff. As for why he wanted them, well, maybe he was trying to tear down the bridge for some reason. He might be one of these kooks who wants to get on the news. If he wasn't a kook, he was probably a crook bribed to do it—or he was doing it for money for some reason. You'd be surprised at how much people will pay for pieces of history."

Alexis elbowed Elizabeth. She was thinking of Dr. Edwards. All of this came down to history.

Cliff ran off to help his crew get the bridge ready for the parade and left the three of them standing staring at the floor.

"Well, I guess I'd better get home," said David.

"Yeah, it's almost dinnertime," said Elizabeth. They all walked toward the front doors. All at once, Alexis stopped and yelled.

"Wait!" cried Alexis. David and Elizabeth spun around in surprise. "David! What are you doing tomorrow?"

"Uh, watching the parade, I guess."

Alexis and Elizabeth exchanged excited glances.

"Do you want to ride with us in the bed race tomorrow?" Alexis asked.

"Please! You have to!" said Elizabeth. "I'm going to push, and Alexis is going to steer, but we don't have a third person!"

"You need a shifter," said David.

"A what?" said the girls together.

"A shifter—someone to sit in the middle of the bed and shift from side to side as you go around corners. It keeps the bed from flipping over. You're in luck. I happen to be the best shifter in Lake Havasu. Been on the winning float two years in a row."

"But that means you raced with Emily!" said Alexis.

"Yeah, I did. Until she broke that guy's arm anyway. She's a good racer, but she's too brutal. She'll do anything to win."

"So you'll ride with us?" asked Elizabeth.

"Of course!" said David. "Where should I meet you?"

"Outside of Bill's Tarnished Treasures first thing in the morning," said Alexis. "Don't forget to wear your costume!"

Alexis walked David and Elizabeth to the sidewalk, where the two of them peeled off in opposite directions—David to his home and Elizabeth to her hotel. Alexis turned to go inside and was almost bowled over by a round man in a flapping suit.

It was the mayor.

"Sorry, girl! Sorry! Didn't see you in all the excitement!"

Then he turned and continued running toward the bridge, yelling at anyone who crossed his path. "Did you hear? Did you hear? The parade is on! There's no curse after all!"

Alexis watched him disappear around the corner, half expecting him to do a hitch kick on his way.

CHAPTER
11
★ ★ ★ ★

The Great Race

The sun was barely up, but the people of Lake Havasu City were already gathering. A variety of beds were ready at the starting line. Racing teams were making final adjustments and getting into position.

Alexis was reattaching a sequined fish that had fallen off when David leaned out over her head from his seat on the bed.

"You almost done?" he asked. Alexis looked up. David's dragon costume was hilarious. It was a glittery blue, and the hood was shaped like a horned dragon's head, complete with three-inch fangs on the front of the snout.

"Yeah, almost," said Alexis. "This fish won't stay put!"

"Well, maybe if your decorations weren't so cheap, they wouldn't fall apart," said a nasty voice from behind them. Alexis spun around and found Emily's knees in her face. They were covered in sparkly tights. Alexis looked up and saw that Emily was dressed like a fairy.

Even her makeup was gorgeous, and she had pointed ears and wings.

"Don't you have your own bed to attend to?" asked David.

"Oh," said Emily to Alexis. "I see you had to pick up last year's leftovers to get a third. Well, good luck, *girls*."

She curtsied to David with her last word and traipsed back to her own bed.

"Don't worry about her," said David as he helped Alexis climb over the wall and onto the bed. "She wouldn't even be talking to us unless she was afraid we might beat her."

"And I think you just might!" It was Bill. He came out of the crowd and hobbled one last time around the castle-bed. "This thing really has a chance with a crew like you three!"

Bill pointed at David and spoke to the girls. "You know this guy's the best shifter in Lake Havasu, right?" he said. "Mary takes the credit. She used to go with his mom to ride go-carts, and she taught him how to take the corners!"

David bowed, his dragon's tail flying up in the air and knocking off Elizabeth's tiara.

"Be careful where you swing that thing!" she said.

"Everybody ready? They're about to start!"

Alexis scrambled to the front and sat in the throne. She twisted her jester's hat so she was looking between two of the floppy arms. There was no way she was going to let a couple of jingle bells keep her from seeing where she was going.

Elizabeth climbed out of the bed and took up her station behind the tower, on the ground. She would be the one to start pushing when the gun went off. David plunked down in between the tower and Alexis's throne. There he would squat, ready to shift to one side or the other each time they took a corner. Hopefully he could keep the bed from tipping up or—even worse—from falling over.

"Alexis! Hey, Alexis!"

Alexis looked over and saw her grandmother's shocking red hair bobbing up and down in the crowd. She was waving frantically, elbowing Dr. Edwards in the side as she did so. He did not seem the least bit interested.

"Hi, Grandma!" called Alexis.

"Drive that thing well, baby!" called Grandma Windsor.

"I will!" cried Alexis. "And I'll meet you at the end of the parade!"

Their conversation was interrupted by the mayor's amplified voice. It roared over the noise of the crowd, causing a hush that was unnatural for so many people. The air hummed, as if the noise was just waiting for the right moment to explode again.

"*Ready! Set!*" called the mayor, the cap gun raised high over his head. *Snap!*

And they were off.

Along the starting line, beds began to roll forward. All of them were slow at first, but after a few seconds they picked up some speed.

"Come on, Elizabeth!" yelled Alexis. Just then David's head appeared over her shoulder.

"Alexis!" he said. "Just around the first corner is a hill! When I tell you to, lean forward as far as you can without falling out!"

"What?" Alexis cried. "What for?"

"You'll see," he said. Alexis didn't like the grin on his face.

The corner came faster than Alexis had expected. They were in the middle of the road with beds on either side. The street curved a little to the right, and David crouched down along the right wall of their castle.

"I'm on!" cried Elizabeth. She had stopped pushing and was now standing on the back of the bed.

"*Now!*" cried David. Alexis leaned forward, keeping her hands on the steering wheel. To her surprise, David was beside her, adding his weight to hers at the front of the bed. Soon she saw why they were doing it.

At first it was only five inches, but soon their castle-bed was a good twenty feet in front of everyone else. Their weight was forcing the bed down the hill faster than all the others!

The wind in her face made Alexis whoop in excitement. *This is how it must feel to fly*, she thought. The road continued straight at the bottom of the hill, so Alexis just sat back in her seat and held tight to the vibrating steering wheel. David returned to the middle of the bed, and Elizabeth got ready to jump off and push—but they were going too fast. She didn't need to.

"Whoo-hoo!" cried Elizabeth. Her head peeked up over the top of the tower. "You guys are doing great!"

"Here comes another corner!" said David. "Alexis! Tap the brakes once, then lean into the turn!" Alexis did as she was told. She tapped the pedal with her foot—but she did it twice. The bed lurched and took the turn at a crawl. They had lost most of their momentum, and two beds flew past them.

"Push, Elizabeth!" called David. Alexis felt the pressure from behind as Elizabeth struggled with the weight of the bed. She could see that the road up ahead dropped off in another hill, and she hoped they could catch up on the way down.

"All right!" shouted David. "Let's do it all over again! Elizabeth—get on! Alexis, lean forward and, no matter what you do, *don't touch the brakes!*"

Once again they were flying. In no time at all they had overtaken two teams. Now only one bed was ahead of them. Alexis looked up and recognized the sparkly wings of Emily's costume.

"We're going to pass her on the curve at the bottom!" said David. "Put our bed on the inside of the turn! Between her bed and the curb! If we lean left, you won't need the brakes! Plus," he said with a smile, "even if we tip, all we'll do is bump her a little. Ready? *Lean!*"

And she did. Alexis leaned to her left with everything she had. The force pulling the bed to the right was crazy. Alexis thought for sure they were going to topple over. Once, their left wheels lifted into the air, but David's weight put them back on the ground.

They came out of the turn just ahead of Emily's bed. An angry screech came from behind them. Then there was a jolt, and their castle-bed almost flew off the road and into the watching audience.

Cheers turned to boos, and after she got control of her bed, Alexis looked over to see Emily passing her.

"Oops!" said Emily. "Guess I got a little close. Sorry!" And she kept rolling.

"No way!" cried Alexis. "She cheated!"

"She always does," said David. "One more curve, then it's a slight hill to the finish. Don't pass her yet. Stay behind her on the turn, and we'll lean down the hill again, okay?"

Alexis nodded. Elizabeth joined them up front. They were going so fast there was no way she could push anymore. The last turn behind them, Alexis gripped the wheel and leaned. David and Elizabeth leaned forward, too, one on either side of her.

They were even with the back of Emily's bed—they were at the middle—they were nose and nose—

The finish line was feet away. Without warning, David put his feet on the castle wall and leaped forward, grasping the finishing ribbon in his hands before falling and rolling beneath the bed with a crash.

Cheers erupted from the crowd. Alexis slammed on the brakes as the medical staff ran out to pull David from under the bed. He was fine, except for some minor scrapes, and one of his dragon's teeth had been knocked out.

"Dragons have tough hides!" he said with a laugh as Alexis and Elizabeth ran up to him.

"That was *crazy*!" said Elizabeth.

"Why did you do that?" asked Alexis.

"I couldn't let her win," he said. "Not like that."

Alexis noticed there was quite a commotion near the side of the finish line. Most of the beds had finished, but the judges seemed to be fighting over something. Alexis led the way over to the judges, her jester's hat flopping in her hands.

"Where's the picture? We have to have the picture!" called one of the judges. He was a short man with a huge mustache.

"It's coming, Wilbur," said another judge. She was tall and was looking around the crowd. "Where's the photographer?" she shouted.

"I'm right here!" called a man in a tweed coat. He was running as fast as he could, huffing from the exertion. A digital camera was around his neck. He stopped near the judges and played with the buttons for a few seconds. Then he passed it to the judges. After a few moments of silence the tall judge spoke.

"I just don't believe it!" she said.

"Me neither," said the little man with the mustache. "But the rules say—"

"The rules say what, exactly?" said Emily. She had abandoned her bed and was stalking toward the judges. "They had better say that I won!"

"Well, actually, young lady," said the man, "you didn't."

He showed her the camera. Emily's mouth dropped open, and she shoved the camera at Alexis. Alexis grabbed the camera. There was the proof, clear as day. David's long arms outstretched, grasping the finish line and beating the front of Emily's bed by a good six inches.

"But their bed didn't cross before mine!" argued Emily. "He jumped off!"

"The rules state that each team member is considered a part of the bed as long as they are touching it," said the lady judge. "And as you can see, his feet were still on the wall when he crossed the finish line."

Emily looked ready to argue, but the mayor burst past her, shoving her to the side.

"Congratulations!" he said, shaking hands with Alexis, Elizabeth, and David. "Great job! New winners!"

He squeezed them all in close, and the photographer took a picture. Then, without a moment to spare, the mayor was gone again.

"The parade!" he called. "Ten minutes until the parade!"

Alexis couldn't believe it. Not only had they been able to race, but they had also won!

"I can't believe we beat Emily!" Alexis exclaimed. "She's so mean that I was sure she'd win!"

"Well, I guess when we do the right thing and try hard, well, maybe the good guys don't always finish last," Elizabeth said. "It's kind of like 2 Samuel 22:25 says, 'The Lord has rewarded me according to my righteousness, according to my cleanness in his sight.'"

The three winners walked through the crowd and found a grassy spot on a hill to watch the parade pass. People kept stopping to congratulate them, and many shop owners told them to come by later for something or other "on the house." They made a plan to get free ice cream and chocolates but *not* to visit the taxidermist who had promised a special surprise.

The parade was all they had hoped it would be. The school marching band opened up, and not far behind them was the golden float from the hotel. Dr. Edwards sat in the driver's seat, accompanied by Grandma Windsor. They were both dressed in authentic costumes from the era of King George III, and Alexis thought it looked like her grandmother was having the time of her life.

You know, she told herself, *Dr. Edwards even looks happy. He looks like a gentleman driving his lady.*

Alexis gasped and stood up.

"What?" asked Elizabeth and David at the same time.

"A gentleman driving his lady," she murmured. "A gentleman. . .driving his *lady*!"

Without explaining, Alexis tore off through the crowd. Elizabeth and David followed, catching up outside the London Bridge Resort.

"What's going on?" Elizabeth panted.

"I think I know where the letter is hidden!" said Alexis. She ran through the automatic doors and stopped. The lobby was empty. Even Jane was nowhere to be seen. Alexis turned toward the golden coach.

"I think I know where it is!" she said again. As she went to cross the red ropes, she tripped, putting out a hand to stabilize herself on the coach. When she touched it, a huge sheet of golden foil came off in her hand.

"Wow," said David. "I thought the replica was sturdier than that!"

Alexis and Elizabeth looked at each other in horror.

"It is," they both said. Then they took off running back out the doors.

"Wait!" called David. "What's going on?"

"It's Dr. Edwards!" said Alexis. "He's stealing the replica from the hotel!"

"How?" asked David. "What are you talking about?"

"You saw the foil slip off," said Elizabeth. "He must have replaced the real carriage with his phony 'float' while everyone was watching the bed race."

"Right now, he's driving the actual replica of the golden carriage through Lake Havasu City!" said Alexis. "And everyone just thinks it's a float!"

The three teens ran across the street and down a couple of blocks. They stopped outside the Lake Havasu City Sheriff's Department. Inside, they met a bored-looking woman sitting at the front desk.

"Excuse me, ma'am," said Alexis. "We have an emergency."

"What is it?" said the woman, sitting up a little straighter and looking alert.

"Someone has stolen the golden carriage from the London Bridge Resort!" said Elizabeth.

The woman behind the desk burst out laughing. She laughed so hard that she began crying. Alexis tried to explain, but the lady just kept laughing and showed them out the door.

Alexis was stupefied. If the police didn't believe them, who would? They walked back slowly to the parade. Grandma Windsor hollered to them, and Alexis pushed her way through the crowd to get to her.

"You're already done, Mrs. Windsor?" asked Elizabeth.

"Yes," Grandma Windsor said. "Dr. Edwards and I were leading the parade, so we were done first. Hey! Why's everybody so glum?"

Alexis didn't think her grandmother would believe her, but there was no reason to hold back anymore. She told her the whole story, from hearing Jerold and Jim in the alley to finding the fake carriage in the lobby only minutes earlier.

"The police don't believe us," Alexis finished. "There's nothing we can do."

"What do you mean, nothing?" cried Grandma Windsor. She disappeared into the crowd, and within minutes honking filled the air. People parted as it came closer. Grandma Windsor was behind the wheel of her cherry red convertible, motioning for Alexis to jump in.

"I don't want to leave you two behind," she said to David and Elizabeth, "but we haven't asked your parents, and we don't have time. I just saw Dr. Edwards loading the carriage into a semitruck. He's already on the interstate, heading west!"

With that they were gone. Alexis buckled her seat belt as Grandma Windsor hit the gas pedal.

"I called the sheriff," said Grandma Windsor. "Told him he'd better listen to me, since he ignored my granddaughter. They should be on their way."

When they got on the freeway, Alexis could barely make out the shape of a truck in the distance.

"It's time to see what this baby can do!"

The engine thrummed as the car went faster. . .and faster.

A siren wailed behind them, and Alexis saw the red and blue of flashing lights in the rearview mirror. *Thank goodness!* she thought. *The sheriff will catch Dr. Edwards in no time!* The car pulled up next to them but didn't drive past. Alexis looked over and gasped.

It was Deputy Dewayne, and he was motioning for Grandma Windsor to pull her car over.

Busted!

"What is he doing here?" hollered Alexis over the noise of the car's engine.

"Well, I did call the sheriff," said Grandma Windsor. "Maybe he wants to question me." She coasted to the side of the road. When the car stopped, Deputy Dewayne pulled in right behind them, lights still flashing and siren blaring.

Grandma Windsor rolled down her window, and Alexis spun around in her seat to watch the deputy approach. He swaggered up to the car and stood with his hands on his hips. The look on his face reminded Alexis of a starving lion that had just found something to eat.

"Ma'am," said Deputy Dewayne to Grandma Windsor, "do you have any idea how fast you were going back there?"

"I'm sorry, Officer," said Alexis's grandma. She put on her best smile. "I must have gotten carried away.

I didn't want the fugitives to get away." Alexis leaned over so she could see Deputy Dewayne's face.

"She's telling the truth, sir," she said. "We were trying to catch up to Dr. Edwards before he gets away with the golden coach."

Deputy Dewayne's eyes narrowed.

"So it's you!" he said. "I should have known!"

"Now Deputy," said Grandma Windsor. "There's no reason to talk to my granddaughter that way." The deputy took off his sunglasses and leaned through the window.

"Now ma'am, you need to understand something," he said. Alexis wondered why he was suddenly talking to her grandmother like she was a five-year-old. "Every time there's been a disturbance this week, I've found this girl in the middle of things."

Grandma Windsor was still smiling, but Alexis could tell that it was getting harder for her to keep it up.

"I'm sure there have been a few misunderstandings," she said, "but that is not the issue right now. Right now we are trying to keep a thief from—"

"I don't think you are qualified to tell me what is or is not the issue, ma'am," said the deputy.

"Maybe not, but if you would just radio the sheriff, he'll tell you—"

Deputy Dewayne stepped back and yanked the car door open.

"Step out of the car, ma'am," he said. Grandma Windsor's mouth dropped open. Alexis dropped her head into her hands with a sigh.

"Don't fight it, Grandma," she said. "This is a losing battle."

Grandma Windsor huffed in anger and got out of her car. Deputy Dewayne spun her around and pulled out his handcuffs.

"Molly Windsor, you're under arrest for obstruction of justice and failure to comply."

Alexis was about to complain when more sirens filled the air. She turned to see four sheriff's cars blow past them on their way to catch Dr. Edwards. Deputy Dewayne stared after them, stunned. He fumbled with Grandma Windsor's handcuffs and ran toward his car. Alexis had a sudden thought. She had to be with the police when they caught Dr. Edwards. She was the only one here who really knew what was going on. But how was she going to get there? Grandma Windsor couldn't drive with her hands cuffed behind her back, and it would be too far to walk. She glanced at Deputy Dewayne and got an idea.

"Um, you'd better take me with you," she said.

"Why would I do that?" he asked suspiciously.

"Well, you said it yourself—I've been involved in every crazy thing that's happened this week. Don't you think I have something to do with this, too?" The deputy opened the passenger door to his car.

"Get in," he said. Alexis smiled at her grandmother as she jumped in the front seat of the police car. She was about to say something when Deputy Dewayne jumped in the other side and took off, siren blazing— and left Grandma Windsor standing in handcuffs on the side of the road.

Neither of them said a word during the drive. Within five minutes they were pulling up behind a gaggle of red and blue lights that had surrounded a huge semitruck. They were just opening the back end when Alexis and Deputy Dewayne walked up.

Alexis saw that Jerold and Jim were already in handcuffs. Alexis watched two officers lead them into one of the patrol cars in front of the truck. The sheriff was near the golden coach, talking to Dr. Edwards. Alexis edged nearer, so she could hear what they were saying.

"I just don't understand it, Doc," said the sheriff. "Why would you steal this thing? What on earth could you do with a replica of a golden coach?"

"Well," said Dr. Edwards, "it's very pretty. Thought it would look good in my garage." He pulled out a handkerchief and blew his nose.

"You expect me to believe that?" said the sheriff. He kept ranting, adding question after question. Dr. Edwards kept answering with one or two words. It was as if he wanted to keep the sheriff talking as long as possible. Alexis got the impression that he was biding time.

"Good, they got him!"

Alexis turned around to see David and Elizabeth standing near her. She looked back and saw Elizabeth's parents wave at her from their car fifty yards behind everyone else.

"How did you know where we were?" Alexis asked.

"When we saw the deputy taking off after your grandma onto the highway, we knew the direction you were going. I called my parents, and they agreed to bring us out."

"So we could be in on the catch!" David said with a big smile.

"Well, *catch* is the right word." Alexis turned to Elizabeth. "Jim and Jerold are up in the front patrol car," she said. Then she explained to David, "Those were the two men who were building the float for Dr. Edwards, the ones we heard talking about the robbery in the alley."

"So what's going on here?" Elizabeth asked, motioning at Dr. Edwards and the sheriff.

"The sheriff's asking questions, like why the doctor stole the carriage, but Dr. Edwards isn't answering them very quickly. I was just thinking that it's almost like he's stalling," she said. And then she realized why he was stalling.

Every few seconds Dr. Edwards scooted a little bit closer to the carriage. He must have known this was his last chance if he wanted to find the document.

"Wait!" cried Alexis. The sheriff spun around, surprised to see her. Dr. Edwards noticed her and gasped. She had never seen his ancient face look so angry.

"Little miss," said the sheriff, "what are you doing here?"

"My grandma was the one who called and told you about the theft," Alexis said. "But it's not really about the carriage at all, is it, Dr. Edwards?" The old professor wiped his nose again.

"Of course it is," he sniveled. "I have no idea what you're talking about, little girl."

Alexis turned toward the sheriff.

"Sir," she said, "Dr. Edwards believes that there is a priceless letter hidden somewhere in the carriage. He came to Lake Havasu City so he could look for it, but when he couldn't find it, he decided to steal the whole carriage instead."

"Is this true?" asked the sheriff, turning toward Dr. Edwards.

Dr. Edwards's lips tightened into a flat line. He was obviously trying not to say anything. When there was no answer, the sheriff turned to Alexis again.

"This is an interesting story," he said. "But there's no evidence that it's true. We've still got him on the theft charge though."

He turned back to Dr. Edwards, as Elizabeth nudged Alexis and showed her something on the cell phone.

Alexis read the words that were texted there and looked up at Elizabeth in amazement. Elizabeth grinned and nodded.

"Sir," said Alexis, touching the sheriff on the elbow. "I know where the letter is hidden—at least I think I do."

Dr. Edwards smirked. "Little girl, I have been searching this carriage for years—visited London Bridge Resort every vacation. There's no way *you* would have been able to find the document after four days in town!"

Alexis ignored him. "May I?" she asked the sheriff.

"Be my guest," he said. Alexis climbed up into the back of the trailer and made her way toward the front of the carriage. A golden wave of water hid the driver's seat from view. When she was level with the seat—where Dr. Edwards had been only this morning—she turned and spoke to the crowd of curious police.

"There's a story that the princess Amelia, King George the Third's youngest daughter, hid a letter for the man she loved in her father's coach. Dr. Edwards was probably looking throughout the inside of the coach, since that's where the princess would have sat, but one of our other mystery-solving friends who loves horses, McKenzie, thought of somewhere else to look. The man the princess loved worked with the horses. In that case she probably would have hidden the note where he would have found it while harnessing them to the carriage."

Alexis grabbed the golden post that was meant to hold the horses and slid her hand into the hollow end. She pulled out a thin box and opened it. The hinges creaked in the silence.

And there it was—a small, folded package, yellowed with age.

"'For the Son of Man came to seek and to save what was lost,'" Elizabeth murmured. "Luke 19:10 doesn't quite fit the situation, but I think God must have nudged McKenzie's brain!"

"No!" hollered Dr. Edwards. "That's mine! Mine by right!"

"How do you figure that, Doc?" asked the sheriff. "And what on earth is a priceless letter doing here, in Lake Havasu City? Shouldn't it be in the real coach in Britain?"

"I did all the research decades ago, while I was in college," said Dr. Edwards. He spoke to the sheriff, but he was glaring at Alexis.

"I finally figured that the letter was probably in the carriage," he continued, "so I wrote to the royal family and got permission to search it from the queen herself. But before I could save the money to go back to Britain, my professor stole my permission letters and went himself. He found the letter, but he told me he had hidden it from the royal family so he could keep it for himself. He died in a train accident on his way to southern California, and it took me fifty years to figure out that he'd hidden it in the carriage. So you see? I did all the work! It's rightfully mine!"

The sheriff smiled sadly.

"It's a sad story, Doc," he said. "And I wish I could take your side, but the truth is that you committed a crime when you stole the replica. Why didn't you just ask permission to search the carriage? We could have helped you take it apart if need be."

Dr. Edwards looked crestfallen. Alexis felt bad for him, but the sheriff was right. Dr. Edwards had committed a crime, and they couldn't reward him by giving him the letter now. Another deputy handcuffed the doctor and led him toward another car with flashing lights.

"I guess we'd better figure out what to do with this," said the sheriff. He stepped forward and reached into the box that Alexis was still holding.

"Stop! Don't touch anything!"

Everyone spun around to see Grandma Windsor leap out of yet another police car. Her wrists had been freed from the cuffs, and she strode toward the back of the truck trailer with purpose, her costume dress flapping behind her.

"You can't just go and grab a two-hundred-and-fifty-year-old document like it was a letter from your mother!" she yelled at the sheriff. The man smiled and stepped back.

"Of course, Professor Windsor. I'm glad you're here. Would you mind helping us out with this?"

"Not at all," Grandma Windsor said with a smile. She slipped a white glove onto her hand and reached into the compartment. She lifted the letter out with a

flat hand and slipped it into a large plastic Ziploc bag.
"It's not perfect, but it will do," she said.

● — ● — ●

The next morning Alexis was sad because it would
be her last day in Lake Havasu City. At least for now.
David and Elizabeth met her in the hotel lobby after
breakfast. David was carrying three neon-colored
rubber duckies.

"What are those for, David?" asked Alexis as he
handed her a pink one. He gave the purple one to
Elizabeth and kept the green one for himself.

"You'll see," he said. "Follow me!"

They left the hotel and made their way toward the
bridge. Alexis noticed quite a crowd gathering along
the railings.

For a moment she was afraid that something was
wrong, but then she realized the people were smiling.

"What's all the commotion?" she asked. "I thought
the festival was over."

"Not quite!" said David. "We close it out with the
duck race!"

Alexis looked at the bridge again and saw that
everyone at the railings had a rubber ducky in their
hands. They were passing the sheriff's department
when Elizabeth grabbed Alexis's arm.

"Look! Wonder where they're taking Jim and Jerold?" she said.

Alexis looked across the street. Two police officers were putting Jim and Jerold into the back of a police car.

"Hey!" said David. "That's the engineer I told you about! The one who wanted the stones from the bridge!" He was pointing to Jim.

"It doesn't surprise me," said Alexis. "Those two were helping Dr. Edwards, but I don't imagine that's the only shady deal they were involved in. I wonder what they wanted them for, if not to destroy the bridge or ruin the race."

"Bet I know what they wanted the stones for," Elizabeth said. "I updated the girls last night on what was going on. Awhile ago Kate texted me that she'd done a search on London Bridge artifacts and found someone selling stones from the London Bridge on several Internet auction sites."

"You mean like eBay?" David asked.

"Well, I'm not sure if it was eBay, but there are a lot of sites out there like that now," Elizabeth said. "One of the sites she saw them on that requires a selling location listed Lake Havasu City. And the sellers' names were words like Jerold, and J and J Auctions."

"We'll have to tell Grandma so she can let the

sheriff know. Then he can look into it," Alexis said.

"Has your grandma found out what's going to happen to the letter from Princess Amelia?" Elizabeth asked.

"Yes, she called the British Museum, and they are super-excited about finally having the letter. They even offered to let Lake Havasu City borrow it each year during the festival," Alexis explained.

Elizabeth looked at David and frowned. "You know there's one other thing I don't get. If it was you making the crack in the bridge, then what was the thing with the old hag cursing the bridge?"

"I know which woman you mean," David said. "That one dressed up to be really ugly? I heard her saying something about the bridge."

"Do you mean Meghan?" Suddenly the young teens realized that Grandma Windsor had joined them. "Are you talking about my friend Meghan?" she asked, linking arms with Alexis.

"I don't know. She was some old lady who looked like she stepped out of the movie *The Princess Bride*," Alexis explained.

"Oh yes, that's Meghan!" Grandma exclaimed. "She's actually not old. She's quite young. She's a drama student who likes to come to the festival dressed up as an old woman. She seems to have a talent for that kind of voice and for living in character. She's great at curses."

"Grandma!" Alexis exclaimed.

"Well, not real curses, silly. They're all make-believe," Grandma said. "She is convincing, isn't she? If she can't make it as an actress, I'm sure she has a future as a makeup artist."

"But she left a message for us," Elizabeth said. "And why would she run away from us if she was your friend?"

"Well, that's just it, dears," Grandma Windsor explained. "I had told her about this fabulous Camp Club Girls you have and all the mysteries you solve. I'm quite proud, you know. She was so afraid you'd be bored that she said she was going to try to stir up a bit of a mystery for you. Secret messages, anyway. She thought it would just be a spot of fun for you."

"You mean you knew all along?" Alexis asked.

"Oh yes, dear. I meant to tell you about it before you thought there was a real mystery there, but it seems like you found your own mysteries to solve without Meghan's help. I think she had a couple of more messages planned, but she had to leave town and go back to where she normally lives—Tuscon, I think.

Her mother got ill and needed her," Grandma Windsor said. "Now Alexis, I need to scoot for a few minutes. I'm on my way to the sheriff's office. Have to see him about that silly ticket his silly deputy gave me. I'll see you at the hotel in a bit."

Grandma Windsor trotted off.

"Well, at least that answers that!" said Elizabeth. "Oh, you know, I decided I'm going to talk to Mr. Bill about buying that spoon with Princess Amelia on it. Mom gave me some money this morning. Alexis, I guess I'm as much of a romantic at heart as you are. I'm going to run and get it and will meet you at the bridge in about ten minutes. Here, hold my ducky for me, will you?" she said as she thrust the purple duck in Alexis's hand.

"So you're a romantic at heart, hmm?" David asked, with a tender smile on his face.

Alexis blushed and shrugged.

"So any chance your grandma will be back in Lake Havasu?" asked David. "Maybe this winter?"

"I don't think so," she said.

"Oh," said David. "I just know some old people like to come to Arizona in the winter. I mean, not like she's old!"

Alexis laughed.

"No, she's not really old," she said. "And I think she's

coming to visit us for the holidays. Dad mentioned a trip up to Tahoe, but I don't think I'll be back down here anytime soon."

"Do you have an e-mail address then?" asked David.

"Better than that," said Alexis. "The Camp Club Girls have a Web site!"

"The *what*?"

"It's a long story," said Alexis. She and David walked to the bridge while she explained to him about the Camp Club Girls and their mysteries. Then Elizabeth joined them, and all three leaned over the railing of the bridge and dropped their ducks into the water.

Alexis didn't know if it was because she had solved two cases, because she was with such good friends, or because God had just erased her fears. But for some reason, she wasn't scared of the bridge anymore.